The
Shark
Attack

Moraa Gitaa

Moran (E. A.) Publishers Limited
Judda Complex, Prof. Wangari Maathai Road,
P.O. Box 30797 - 00100, Nairobi

With offices and representatives in: Uganda, Rwanda, Tanzania, Malawi
and Zambia

www.moranpublishers.com

Text © Moraa Gitaa, 2014
Design and illustrations © Moran (E. A.) Publishers Limited, 2014

ISBN 978 9966 34 738 1
ebook ISBN 978 9966 63 222 7

2017   2016   2015   2014
8   7   6   5   4   3   2   1

FOREWORD

The National Book Development Council of Kenya (NBDCK) is a Kenyan non-governmental organization made up of stakeholders from the book and education sectors. It promotes the love of reading, the importance of books and the importance of quality education.

The Burt Award for African Literature project involves identification, development and distribution of quality story books targeting the youth, and awarding the authors. It is funded by Bill Burt, a Canadian philanthropist, and implemented by the NBDCK in partnership with the Canadian Organization for Development through Education (CODE).

The purpose of the Burt Award books such as *The Shark Attack* is to give the reader high quality, engaging and enjoyable books whose content and setting are portrayed in an environment readers can easily identify with. This sharpens their English language and comprehension skills leading to a better understanding of the other subjects.

My profound gratitude goes to Bill Burt for sponsoring the Burt Award for African Literature in Kenya. Special thanks also go to the panel of judges for their dedicated professional input into this project. Finally, this foreword would be incomplete without recognizing the important role played by all NBDCK stakeholders whose continued support and involvement in the running of the organization has ensured the success of this project.

Ruth K. Odondi
Chief Executive Officer
National Book Development Council of Kenya

ACKNOWLEDGEMENT

The Burt Award for African Literature recognizes excellence in young adult fiction from African countries. It supports the writing and publication of high quality, culturally relevant books and ensures their distribution to schools and libraries to help develop young people's literary skills and foster their love for reading. The Burt Award is generously sponsored by a Canadian philanthropist, Bill Burt, and is part of the ongoing literacy programs of the National Book Development Council of Kenya, and CODE, a Canadian NGO supporting development through education for over 50 years.

Chapter One

Big Man signaled his henchmen by holding his right palm near his right ear, struck it with his left palm and at the same time flicked his head sideways over the right seaboard side of the ship towards the high seas. When Kadzo saw the familiar gesture, she knew that she, her brother, Kenga, and their friend, Issa, were in trouble. They had seen this gesture before and someone's life had been snuffed out. She was glad that they were still in their flippers and swim gear, and if push came to shove, they could strike for the beach.

Suddenly, as if in response to Big Man's unspoken command, one of the burly stevedores lunged at Kadzo and grabbed her T-shirt front, which she had put on over her swimsuit. Just then, a loud explosion went off at the helm of the mother ship. The impact threw everyone overboard as the vessel burst into flames.

* * *

Finding herself in the deep sea, Kadzo started treading water, thanking God that she, Kenga and Issa, were all good swimmers. She wondered what on earth had made them trust the drug cartels and join them time and again aboard their ship. She realised then that this was not the *Pirates of the Caribbean* and none of the stevedores aboard the gang's second ship anchored nearby was going to shout, 'Man over board!' Instead, the men in the second ship lifted anchor, opting not to rescue their colleagues in the ocean. The ship started drifting away.

Kadzo watched from a distance as she paddled water with her hands. The first ship they had been on disintegrated into a vast ball of flames. Splinters of metal, wood and debris rose on the back of a mushroom-like cloud and drifted lazily into the air as if suspended in slow motion. It then fell back into the ocean in a cascade of foamy, white splashes. Finally, the smoke evaporated into a single wall several feet high above the surface, then vanished into the air. Horrified, Kadzo stared at the spot where they had anchored Safari Hatua, their brand new Chris-Craft speedboat. They were to use it to transport the cargo back to Kinango. Safari Hatua was nowhere to be seen. Kadzo looked around, trying to locate the boat but she could not see it.

"The boat must have drifted further off into the high seas," she thought. They will have to search for her later. She suddenly noticed Big Man and the two stevedores on a lifeboat from a distance – the goons had managed to salvage the life-saving raft from the burning ship and escaped death. The men did not seem interested in looking for the young kids in the vast ocean. They rowed off in the direction of the second freighter.

Kadzo glanced around as she cut through the water to make sure that Kenga and Issa were with her. She could not see them in the vast ocean. She sensed that something was terribly wrong.

Kadzo could feel it in her guts. A deep sense of foreboding engulfed her. The jetty and pier were too far off to the left. She glanced at her diver's water- proof watch as she treaded the water. It was almost 4:00 p.m. They had spent too much time on the mainland that day. They needed to be heading back to the island – they had to be home by 7:00 p.m. otherwise, their parents would wonder where they had been, as it was a school day.

Kadzo could see the outline of the Arabuko Sokoke Forest in the distance. This tourist attraction lay on one extreme end of the silvery beach, and on the other end, the towering coconut trees among the tall mangrove stalks stood as if telling her, You must swim upto where I stand. Kadzo looked at the forest with apprehension. Many white people frequented the forest to have a glimpse of the numerous birds, animals and butterflies but she also knew that the forest held many secrets. She had been there so many times, collecting or delivering cargo. Kenga and she had been there a few weeks ago and they had earned handsomely from the transaction.

* * *

Kadzo decided to swim towards the beach. The only sound she could hear was the faraway crash and hiss of the waves breaking on the hard, wet sand and the plaintive cries of the white-winged seagulls skimming the waters, and the whistling African eagles that had perched on the trees of the Arabuko Sokoke. Her rhythmic handstrokes in perfect freestyle propelled her towards the distant beach-line. A tingle of unease crept up her spinal cord again.

3 ◀

She wondered where Kenga and Issa were. She did not want to imagine what would possibly have happened. The tide was becoming more hostile and their beloved Safari Hatua was nowhere in sight. The onset of the Easterly Harmattan winds from across the Sahara seemed to have arrived a week ahead of schedule. The strong undercurrents seemed to overwhelm her in such a way that she found herself pushed to the opposite direction, not where she was headed to.

A speedboat with two young African men, one at the wheel and the other being pulled behind on skis, glided past the debris of the wrecked ship on the starboard side which was now engulfed in a huge ball of fire. Kadzo waved to them, hoping they could rescue her, but their boat was speeding. They did not even slow down to look at the burning ship.

Kadzo tried to avoid the white churning waters in the speedboat's wake, coming crosswise towards her but there seemed to be very little she could do to prevent the white turbulent waters from pushing her further into the sea. As she was wrestling with the water, a huge grey shape drifted beneath her, blotting out the sea bed. She did not give it much attention as her interest was on pulling herself through the turbulent water to the shore. After stabilising herself, she glanced behind her and spotted Kenga. His arms were flailing and flapping as if he was struggling. She wondered because Kenga was the only one able to beat her in local swimming galas – but only occasionally and only in the backstroke style.

Suddenly, Issa, who was the poorest swimmer of the trio, flashed past both Kenga and Kadzo. He swam on towards the beach until his feet touched the shallow sea bed. He started yelling and gesturing at Kadzo and Kenga. Kenga was now a few metres behind her.

Kadzo tried to make out the words that Issa was shouting. At first she could not make sense of the words because the sounds were carried away by the strong wind.

"*Papa! Papa!*" Issa kept shouting over and over again until he was out of breath.

Finally, Kadzo deciphered the words. A shark!

"*Yaa Allâh!*" she thought. "The dark shape that passed beneath me! It was a shark!"

She did not look back again but swam for her life like she had never done before. She was not the only one who cared about her life. Kenga emerged from behind and for the first time, beat Kadzo at freestyle. He swiftly swam past her, leaving her in his wake.

It was then that Kadzo understood why a few minutes earlier Kenga seemed to have been struggling – the shark must have entangled itself between his legs as it swam for a prey. In a moment, Kadzo was faced with a serious challenge. She thought she was entangled in seaweeds, when she saw a large shape on her left hand side turn sharply and a dark triangle-like fin slice the water. She knew it immediately. It was the shark.

Kadzo swam frantically towards the beach which now seemed impossibly distant. Her flippers churned the water behind her and her arms flailed as she struck desperately for the distant shore about three hundred metres away. She wished that a dolphin would come by. She longed for the friendly mammal she had played with as they frolicked in the sea at Wasini Island when fishing there with their father. How she wished the dark shape was a dolphin but the fin she had seen dimmed her wishes. She glanced up and saw that Kenga and Issa had made it safely to the beach. She knew that they could not risk coming back to try and rescue her.

As Kadzo flailed against the strong current, she felt the shark head butt her twice and then a huge clamp close around her left leg. The pain was excruciating. She screamed. The shark yanked her below the water surface, swung and jerked her through the water like a piece of damp sea weed. Instinctively, her right hand lunged down and grappled over the shark's tough skin until she felt the soft hollow of the shark's eye socket and tore it with her fingers. The huge clamp loosened, albeit momentarily. Kadzo remembered what she had recently read in the newspaper about a young girl who had been attacked by a crocodile while fetching water from the Tana and how she had fought back by trying to gouge out the reptile's eyes, an action that saved her life.

Kadzo broke to the surface screaming and gasping for air. She looked back, but the shock kept her from comprehending what she saw. The flipper that had been on her left foot was not there. Stuck out below her severed calf muscle, just below the knee, was a white bone. It was snapped off as if sliced by their neighbour butcher, Rashid's knife.

"Oh my God!" she sighed. The shark had bitten off her lower left leg! All around her, the emerald-green water turned red with her blood. She knew the pain she was feeling could have been worse but it had been dulled by the salty sea water. She kept moving, though very slowly.

The bull shark continued chewing the chunk with its head on the water surface. Then it closed in for a second attack. It swam past Kadzo, made a slight turn and confronted her from the front; its tail lashing the water and its body looped round in a u-shape, it moved closer. Its huge jaws took a hold of Kadzo's right leg. The shark's huge, muscular body flexed and swung round behind Kadzo and up along her on the other side, swinging her to and fro like a wet rag and then tossed her into the air. As the force hit her and threw her up into the air, she felt like she had been hit by a truck. She landed onto the water surface painfully. The shark got hold of her again. Its strong jaws with three rows of seven centimetre long and razor-sharp triangular teeth, snapped repeatedly, fighting to get a better grip on its helpless and hapless victim.

Even though in pain, Kadzo thought of the bottlenose dolphins of Wasini again. They were not there to save her. She wished that the friendly mammals would appear from nowhere and form a protective wall around her and drive the shark away.

Another sting struck and she came back to her senses. The shark's teeth tore through her right calf, slicing tendons, arteries and muscles down to the bare bone. Kadzo managed to rise to the surface and screamed for help again.

"Help! Help me!" She waved her hands in the direction of the beach but decided to save her energy and fight off the shark when she realised that her screams were being blown away by the strong winds. She got a grip of herself and thought: "If a nine-year-old girl on the Tana could fight for her life alone, why not me?"

Trying to paddle the water with her left hand alone, which was extremely difficult, she reached down with her right; lunging, plunging, squeezing and tearing at the shark with all her strength. The monster was now trying to tear off her right leg too! She felt the shark's thick skin on the sloping forehead and further down, the softer fold of skin around the eye. She dug in, clawing with her fingers again and again. Sooner than later, she felt the mighty jaws relax and release their grip. Kadzo saw the shark swim away from her. Its fin slicing the water as it left behind fresh trails of blood – her blood! She tried to kick the water and dash to the beach but she could feel neither leg.

"Oh my God!" she thought. "They're gone! *Allâh*! Help me! Save my life and I'll never skive classes again and never ever use or peddle drugs again. Help me *Allâh*!" She prayed deliriously.

Then she saw a small *mashua* draw near her and before long; she slipped into a coma. She could see strange faces and one that looked like Kenga's peer at her over the side of the dhow. Soon strong hands lifted her out of the water.

* * *

Startled, Kadzo woke up with a start from her now recurring nightmare and sat up in bed, shaking and sweating. She reached down and felt her left leg. The healing stump was swaddled in bandages and the gauze had taken the place of her leg. It was not a dream – she had indeed lost her left leg in the shark attack a couple of weeks ago. She was now a cripple. The surgeons had been forced to amputate what was left of the leg from the knee. At least, they had been able to save her right leg. She looked around her – it was a familiar surrounding. She was still at the rehabilitation centre. A sick stomach made her retch. She vomited the breakfast she had been served earlier by the kind nurse aide. She felt some kind of stickiness and wetness on the hospital bed sheets and frowned. She had done this on herself, again!

She had seen people suffer when denied cocaine or heroin but she had never imagined that she could also go through the same. She had seen them tremor, wade in mud in a bid to cool the body, undress and mutter incoherent speeches like people out of the world and somehow she never understood them. It was now her turn. The symptoms that had been the order of the day for the past two weeks were back with a vengeance. She longed for just a pinch of the white powder, to sniff and get better, or a little heroin to inject herself with and get hold of herself again but all this was not available here.

The healing stump that was all that had remained of her left leg started to ache, the pain mixing mercilessly with tremors in her nerves. The throbbing pain made her reach for the bell on the headboard frantically. She wanted to call the nurse for a painkiller. Unfortunately, she underestimated the distance between herself and the bell. Alas! She fell off the bed and landed on the cold tiled floor with a thump and jarring pain. She wondered why that had happened yet she always had a perfect vision like the eagle's. Damn it, denial! There was nobody to help her get back into bed. The beds on either side were empty as the two occupants had been discharged the previous day. She screamed out aloud and dragged herself to the corner of the empty ward. Torrents of tears continued flowing down her cheeks. The nurses came and helped her up. The nurse aide who had attended to her earlier looked at her pitifully and informed her that she would be having a visitor later in the day.

That afternoon, Kenga and Issa walked in. They were in the company of Amina, chatting freely as if they were long time friends. Kadzo was lying on the bed, staring into the space as if in deep thought. Kenga rushed to his sister's side, while Amina took the only chair in the room. Issa stood near the door.

"I am keeping guard," Issa joked.

"My name is Amina, I am a friend to all young people and have been given permission to talk to you. Kadzo, how are you feeling?" Amina started off.

"Much better," Kadzo replied smiling sheepishly. Amina's friendly face made her feel better.

"Accidents do happen and I know that the shark attack was not your fault. You don't need to blame yourselves," Amina helped Kadzo and the boys feel comfortable but the kids could still feel the unspoken words in her voice. 'Although skipping classes to play truant was purely your fault and I also don't condone that.'

They appreciated her offer of friendship and encouraged her to stay with them. Amina spoke to the kids and had them tell her their secrets.

"Tell me," she said now sounding very serious, "do you just transport the drugs or you also use them?"

"I do both. I have been using cocaine and heroin," Issa spoke up, glad to talk to someone who was ready to be his friend. Amina was impressed by Issa's openness; Kenga looked at Amina sheepishly and then dropped his eyes.

"I too. Though I really want to stop."

"Me too," Kadzo added.

Amina did not show any reaction. She was glad that her new friends trusted her. She got some fliers from her folder and showed them pictures of drug addicts. The kids could not believe where they were headed to. The people looked scary. Their hair was unkempt and their nails long and dirty. The children wondered whether 'powder' would reduce someone to bare bones and turn their healthy skin to scales and scabies. Each of the people in the pictures had scabies on their skin. The dirt that had accumulated on them made it barely recognisable as human skin. Some did not have a single tooth.

The three looked at Amina unbelievingly. Her eyes told them all. "If you continue using drugs you are on the downward spiral to becoming like the people in the pictures; you are courting death." Kadzo saw Amina's pupils narrow as they drove the point to their every nerve. Kenga seemed to read Amina in the same way. Issa remained calm. He did not blink.

"We never thought that our indulgence would affect us and other people. I am very sorry for getting Kenga into this. I must get clean and overcome this menace," Kadzo said, throwing blows at an imaginary shark with her clenched fists.

After some conversation, Amina handed her card to Kadzo and told her that they could call her any time if they needed to talk to someone. She then left the room and went to the doctor's office.

Chapter Two

The sight was shocking. Kenga did not think he would be able to bear the pain that Kadzo was feeling. His elder sister was huddled in a corner of the makeshift rehabilitation ward. She was trembling and shaking terribly. The sheets on the tiny cot were covered in human waste. He looked at her sorrowfully. He dreaded the process although he knew that it was inevitable for him. He imagined that his would not be as painful as Kadzo's as she had been in the habit longer than him.

Again, Kadzo started retching. She vomited all over the floor. Their mother stroked her corn-row hair tenderly and tried to lift her up but she resisted and struggled. She did not like this. She detested the fact that her mother was seeing her in that state. Issa, his sister Jamila and their parents were transfixed. They were wondering whether that was part of the recovery and whether Issa would cope with it. The three Abduls looked at Issa and a film of tears formed in their eyes. Issa looked down and curved his shoulders inward; no one uttered a word. The doctor who walked in interrupted their thoughts when he beckoned them to follow him.

"Please, I think you've seen enough," he said once they were in his office. "Those are what we call withdrawal symptoms and they even kill the weak, especially because of the excess vomiting and passing of loose stool. You've not seen anything yet, sometimes, in extreme cases of diarrhoea, the intestines poke out," the doctor said as he looked at Kenga and Issa as if asking, 'Are you ready to go through that?'

"Kenga, your sister has decided to be clean and that is why she is determined to complete the process," the doctor finally said after scrutinising Kenga.

At that point Dr Abdul, Issa's father interrupted, "Thank you very much, Doctor. I would like you to tell us more about all this mess before we can take the next step. He implored. "I'm a general practitioner and I don't have all the facts about drug and substance abuse… and what I can do to help my son, Issa."

Dr Otieno looked at Issa and then shifted his eyes to his parents. He beckoned them to the window of his office. They all stared at the busy street outside the county hospital.

"As you well know, this is not the best rehabilitation centre. It is only a temporary one, set up by the government to try and combat this drug addiction crisis that is beating our country," he said as he fixed his eyes on a group of young men and women at a corner on the street. He shook his head as if not sure of what he wanted to say.

"I can recommend a few excellent rehabilitation and detox centres where your son can get good group therapy sessions," the doctor said as his index finger pointed at the youth. "He needs therapy because this town is littered with drugs and the peddlers are everywhere."

"Once rehabilitated, he'll need to be very strong so as not to relapse into the habit. Do you see those vendors and hawkers out there?" He asked pointing at the hawkers outside. "Most of them are peddling drugs. Look at that young man there selling sweets and magazines that are hidden under his arm? He's the most notorious one. The cops know it, but there he is, free."

After scrutinising the hawkers, they all went back to the seats they had occupied before they had gone to the ward to see Kadzo.

"I understand that you kids have also been peddling drugs and acting as couriers for some drug barons," the doctor said, looking at Issa and Kenga. "Is that why Kadzo was attacked by the shark?" The boys looked down. "Anyway, the worst case scenario that is causing nightmares for the security intelligence is that narcotics mix with organised crimes, like prostitution and illegal arms, making it difficult to control. There is lack of a clear policy on rehabilitation in many countries, and Kenya is no exception."

"Doctor, do you want to say that there is no hope for our children?" Mr Karisa asked, his voice filled with worry.

"No, I don't mean that," Dr Otieno said. "What I would like you to know is that rehabilitation alone is not enough. One needs to make a personal decision to resist the temptations as these drugs have infiltrated the community to a great extent. Children today are not only smoking bhang but also mixing it with heroin. That's why it has a funny smell nowadays!" He shook his head after staring at the street outside in silence. "The fight is a daunting one," he continued. "Rehabilitated drug addicts should be given a chance to engage in productive activities but that's not happening here. Unfortunately, most of them fall back because of frustration," he said eventually spilling his worries.

"The anti-narcotics bosses are lone rangers fighting many forces," he said. It is an open secret that most of the drug barons in the country are big names and they are in high places," he concluded.

"So what's the way forward?" Mr Karisa, Kadzo and Kenga's father who had joined them asked. Dr Otieno looked pensive.

"I've talked to Kadzo and she is what I would call a 'functional addict," he said as he adjusted his spectacles.

"Most of these children have become 'functional addicts', but remain unaffected by the addiction because their systems can regulate the substances they ingest and appear very normal to their gullible parents," he said looking at Mr Karisa as if repremanding him for not making an effort to understand his daughter.

"That is what Kadzo is – a functional addict," the doctor said, shaking his head as if whatever he said was a mystery. This kind of addicts indulge in drugs just to conform to their friends but they know when to stop."

"Most families are enablers and supporters," Dr Otieno said, throwing a glance at Dr Abdul.

"They enable their children's addictions by pretending that there is nothing wrong with them," he continued. "An example is when a parent who is not well-off does not question the kids when they come home with expensive toys," he said as he took off his spectacles and started wiping them with a piece of cloth.

"To come to our earlier discussion, Dr Abdul, you are a wealthy man and I suggest that you book Issa into an exclusive clinic located near the foot of Mount Kenya," the doctor said in a tone stressing this as the only way Issa could be rehabilitated. "There, he will be treated with conventional medicine which will act as a substitute for the hard drugs. I guarantee you, that this will help him to clean up his act."

"Can you promise me, Doctor that this will happen?" Dr Abdul asked looking at Dr Otieno. "I am ready to do anything to help Issa quit the habit."

"Yes, but he has to be willing to reform, like Kadzo," Dr Otieno said. "It is almost impossible to help them if they are not willing to help themselves," he said swinging in his chair again." As for you Mr and Mrs Karisa, you have pointed out that you can't afford private clinics. We shall have to do our best here to liberate Kadzo and Kenga." The parents bowed in complete gratitude to the doctor for his concern for their children.

Dr Abdul stood up and shook hands with Dr Otieno as he led the party out of the children doctor's clinic.

* * *

In half an hour's time, they were in the principal's office at Washa-Washa School where Issa, Kadzo and Kenga attended. The principal called Issa, Kadzo and Kenga's class teachers to join them.

"We are really sorry that it had to come to this, Kenga and Issa," the principal said addressing the boys, "I hope that you've both learnt a lesson from this tragedy. We've warned you many time, but you have not listened to us," the principal said.

"Yes. I've learnt my lesson and I'm very sorry," Kenga said, his eyes fixed on the floor. "I'm willing to corrct my mistakes."

"Many parents have this misconception that by sending their children to school they have ceased their role in the upbringing of those children," she said with a firm voice. "They are wrong. Drugs have found their way into schools and more so in boarding schools where the situation is indeed worse," the principal continued.

"Some of you students in this school come from very rich homes and even own some of the latest models of cars and cell phones…and we are left to wonder…" She did not want to continue.

Dr Abdul cleared his throat and said, "I now realise that some of us parents are to blame; we give our children more than they need although we have no time to supervise them and to show them how they should spend what we give them. I regret that's how they end up in drugs."

"Other children, like my own, are from poor families," Kadzo's father butted in as if from sleep. "Poverty and the need to be like their rich peers lead them into drug peddling."

He turned to Issa and Kenga thoughtfully and addressed them sternly.

"You have always been at the top of your classes; I do not see how you can remain at the top of your class unless you stop using and peddling drugs and concentrate on your studies."

Dr Abdul remembered how hostile he had been the first time Issa's class teacher had raised his concerns. He remembered how he had told the teacher and the principal not to envy his son as he had all he wanted because he could afford it. Now, he regretted it. He was so much in thought that he did not hear the principal ask whether they had any plans for Issa, whom the school thought needed serious rehabilitation.

"That's why we've come over," Mrs Abdul said interrupting her husband's thoughts. "We have come to apologise and request for some time off for Issa so that we can book him into a rehabilitation centre."

"That's fine with me," the principal said as she stood up to escort the two families out of her office.

Chapter Three

B ack at his office, Dr Abdul sat pensively. He stood and paced up and down for several minutes. He turned abruptly from the window and the young people running their errands on the street, and went back to his seat. He tiredly massaged his temples with his thumbs. Resting his elbows on his desk, he sighed dispiritedly and made a steeple with his fingers. This was a nightmare. He remembered the day it had all begun.

A hesitant knock on the door drew an impatient sigh from Dr Abdul's lips. "Come in," he had called out. Sister Ann shut the door behind her.

"Yes, Sister. What is it?" he asked. "I'm looking at my next patient's file. I only have a few minutes. What brings you over from OP?" he said, his slight Indian accent colouring his speech.

"Um…there's been an accident," sister Ann said. "I think you should come with me. Your son witnessed a very bad accident. He and another boy have brought the victim to the hospital, and although Issa and his friend Kenga are not hurt, they are in shock. The girl, Kadzo, has lost a leg." The doctor threw a cursory glance at his wrist watch.

"I think you are mistaken. Issa is still at school," the doctor replied, getting back to his file. After a couple of minutes, he became aware that the nurse was still in the room.

He adjusted the rimless spectacles on the bridge of his nose and stared intently at Sister Ann.

"Well?" he intoned.

"It's not a mistake, Doctor; I know Issa and his friends very well. They've been brought in from the South Coast. A shark attack!"

"*Vot!? Vot* are you saying? I don't understand ... how?" he stammered as he usually did whenever he was distressed.

"Please, just come with me, Doctor. I think you should see them. Your presence will calm the boys. They are in shock."

Dr Abdul hurriedly instructed his nurse aide to assign his patients to another doctor. They left the inpatient block where his consulting rooms were situated and headed to the main building. Abdul was usually level-minded but at the moment, his mind was in turmoil. "A shark attack. How?"

As he walked along the sanitised corridors, he kept nodding his head in acknowledgement to several greetings, oblivious of who the well wishers were. Sister Ann went to resume her work in the theatre after ensuring that Dr Abdul was with the boys.

Abdul came up short when he recognised Mr and Mrs Karisa.

"You! I should have known your children *vill* be involved in this! *Vot* on earth have they gotten my son into this time?" he thundered.

"Don't you dare come here and insult us!" Mr Karisa said, standing up." We all know it's Issa who has the car and the money. They go where they want and do whatever they want."

"What about that expensive speedboat that your children own?" Dr Abdul shouted back."Isn't that what makes them cut classes for their jaunts at sea?"

"At least the boat was a present," Mr Karisa answered, becoming livid. "What about Issa's Harley-Davidson motorbike?"

"*Nyamazeni nyinyi nyote,*" Kadzo's mother said calmly, interrupting the two. She then turned to address Dr. Abdul, "*Wewe wampatia mtoto gari na maelfu ya pesa. Sisi ndio maskini na huyo mtoto wenu ndiye anayewaharibu wanangu, Kadzo na Kenga. Sasa mwanangu Kadzo hana mguu. Yuafanyiwa opresheni, hata anaweza akaaga dunia...*"

She convulsed in sobs and almost passed out. Her husband held her shuddering shoulders and helped her to sit down. Dr Abdul was shattered by Mrs Karisa's words.

"Oh my God!" Dr Abdul said. "*Vea* is Issa and Kenga?" He asked no one in particular.

"They've been given sedatives and are resting," Mr Karisa answered.

Dr Abdul took out his cell phone and walked outside to make calls. He placed several short calls. He talked to his wife and daughter, explaining what had happened and reassured them that Issa was alright. He then came back and took his seat in the waiting room.

Half an hour later, his wife, Sonia, walked in. She was adorned in riches. Her jewellery of diamonds set into filigree threads of gold and silver twisted together said volumes about how much she owned. Her silk *sare* caught the eyes of the worried fathers and mother. Soon, the doctor arrived from the theatre and briefed the parents about Kadzo's welfare. No sooner had Dr Otieno left the waiting room than Abdul's daughter, Jamila, walked in. She also exuded the same aura as her mother. She rushed to her mother and hugged her tightly.

"Oh my God!" She said as she scanned the room to take note of those that were present. "Mother, what happened?"

"Where is Issa?" Mother held daughter for a while and then looked deep into her eyes and shook her head.

"Jamila, you've been right all along," Mrs Abdul said releasing her daughter and stooping. He has been taking drugs."

"Please, forgive us for not paying attention to your suspicions," she wiped a tear from her eyes with her index finger then continued, " I can't believe I've been so blind!"

Jamila looked at her father. Dr Abdul was seated with his head in his hands.

"So where are they? Can we go and see them?" Jamila asked her mother. "I only took an hour off from work."

Mrs Abdul took her daughter's arm and the others followed her.

* * *

Kenga and Issa sat up on their beds when the door was pushed open. Issa's mother went and hugged her son and started crying over his shoulders.

"How could you, Issa? *Vat* on earth were you thinking?" These were the first words that left Dr Abdul's lips. "Is this your *vay* of aiming for your medical degree?"

"Please, I think we should give them a chance to explain," Mrs Abdul interrupted. "Issa, can you tell us what happened?"

Jamila went and sat beside her brother and took his hand in hers. Issa explained everything slowly as Kenga interjected now and then. What followed the narration was a deathly silence in the room.

"So, why were you at the South Coast?" Jamila asked.

"Last week, the TV news showed a footage near Ocean Front Restaurant where some boys were caught by the police taking drugs," Kenga offered to explain. "Some tried to escape by swimming across the channel but one of them drowned. That's why we changed our hideouts and have been hanging out at the South Coast. We've also been meeting the suppliers of the drugs there," he went on. "Today, they seemed to have a fallout. That's when the explosion occurred and we were thrown overboard."

"Issa! You could have died!" his mother said while stroking his cheek.

"Thank God, you're still with us."

"Can you tell us how you get these drugs," Dr Abdul said thoughtfully. "In fact, I'd like to know when you got yourself trapped in this mess," he shook his head, revealing the agony in his heart. "I really blame myself because your sister tried to warn us that you were not yourself but we wouldn't listen to her."

"I wish you had," Issa muttered under his breath.

"What did you just say?" Dr Abdul asked incredulously.

"…Listened to Jamila. I badly needed help. I tried to stop in vain…," his speech slurred. He shuddered. Obviously, the memory of the shark attack had gripped him.

"Dad, Mum, Jamila, please, forgive me," he eventually said, envisioning the ship on fire and the shark tearing Kadzo. "I did not know that I would find myself locked in this behaviour and witness such a terrible thing as what happened today."

"The first time I smoked bhang, it made me feel high in a good way. I became unusually relaxed." He opened his arms as if to fly then went on. "I continued to do this little by little and with time, I realised I was a regular and wanted more and more." He turned and looked away. "That's when I talked to Kadzo and Kenga and discovered that they were way ahead. They were not only using the drug but peddling them. They brought some Valium and D-5 for me. Soon I was into mandrax. Sooner than later, I realised that mandrax too wasn't enough for me," Issa said.

"I was always seeking stuff harder than what I was already taking and that's how I ended up on cocaine and *kikete* (heroin). The rest is history."

Everybody in the room was stunned by the revelation. Most of all, Kenga's parents, when he took up from where Issa had stopped.

"It's very easy for us to get the stuff," Kenga added. "It's sold all over town, especially in our hood in the Old Town. In fact, Issa is the one who introduced us to all our customers there.

Roche 10 in the Old Town is child's play," he wiped his hands in demonstration.

"We have even graduated to being couriers ourselves. That's why we've been meeting up with the suppliers in the deep seas," he concluded. "The demand is high."

Issa's father moved forward and held his son's hand. "Oh my God!" he exclaimed as he lifted Issa's hand to the light and stared at the faded needle marks on his arm, some were still fresh. Mrs Karisa also took Kenga's arm and scrutinised it for needle pricks.

"Mum!" Kenga cried. "You know I've always been scared of injections! I've been sniffing and snorting mine," Kenga said.

"Oh, *Allâh* no!" Mrs Abdul was shocked. She sat on the edge of one of the beds with her head in her hands. Jamila, who was starting to feel slightly nauseous, went over to her mother and held her shoulders.

"Can we go home now, please?" Jamila asked. "I've had enough of hospital for the day," she said as she rose up.

"We'll come and see Kadzo later."

Mrs Abdul and Jamila walked out of the room while Dr Abdul went to consult the doctor who had first treated the boys for shock. He waited to follow up on the progress of the operation on Kadzo's legs. The Karisas remained behind thinking about what had befallen their son and daughter.

Chapter Four

Kenga sat outside their house in the Old Town near Fort Jesus on an old overturned dhow. He was in a trance-like state. He was engrossed in the thoughts about the day he had almost lost his sister in the shark attack. It had been horrific. The thought of how the shark had almost caught him and how it had managed to get his poor sister caused his heart to beat faster. He and Issa had watched from the beach in shock and disbelief as Kadzo fought frantically between life and death. The highness of the cocaine they had snorted earlier on had worn off because of shock.

He and Issa had run up and down the beach alerting the local fishermen who were mending their nets, sorting and gutting the day's catch in their canoes. The fishermen, oblivious of the calamity that had befallen the kids, were at first reluctant to assist. They feared it could be a bad omen and that they might offend the gods from the forest. However, they agreed to help them when they saw tears flowing from one of the boys' eyes. They also saw someone struggling in the sea from afar and gave in to the boys' request.

The fishermen tightened the knots on their *kikois* and got into their boats with Issa and Kenga. As soon as they got to Kadzo, Kenga could see that she was already drifting in and out of consciousness. He had wondered whether the shark was still around waiting for her to die before it could have a whole meal. Their grandfather had once told them how the smell of blood draws sharks closer. This worried him. The fact that bull sharks were known to hunt in twos also brought in more fears. The fishermen had approached with their dhows, churning the waters to ensure there were no sharks underneath. They then carefully pulled their boat towards Kadzo. Kabili, the most experienced of the fishermen kept watching the water for any ripples that might be moving towards them. There was none. He whistled and the team moved to work.

The strong hands of the fishermen lifted Kadzo out of the water and into the boat. The minute she was lifted out of the water, the dull leaden weakness seeping through her body was replaced by incredible pain – she had screamed aloud, throwing her hands up and about. She became so delirious that she almost passed out.

They had managed to save Kadzo from the water but not all was well with her. What Kenga saw made him feel pain; a pain almost equivalent to what his sister was probably feeling. He could not imagine that Kadzo's left leg had been ripped off by the shark. For some seconds, he just stared at her. He had been thrown between hopelessness and hopefulness but he thanked God silently that she was still alive and her right leg was intact though badly mutilated. A woman saw them and rushed to her *makuti*-thatched hut, her hands on her head. She came back with several *lesos*.

Kenga wrapped Kadzo's legs in the *lesos* hoping to stem the bleeding. They also wrapped her whole body in extra *lesos* to keep her warm. The fishermen helped the two boys carry Kadzo up the cliffs and rugged coral rocks to the main road where they flagged down a passing car. Kenga had gently talked to his sister telling her to try and keep calm as they were trying to save her life.

Thoughts of a neighbour who used to dive for seafood for a local marine company occupied Kenga's mind – he had been bitten by a baby shark and had actually died due to excessive bleeding. He could hear the voice of the fishermen punctuating the humid air as they walked away.

"Hawa watoto wa matajiri ni watoro shuleni, wanakuja huku mbali kujificha, wavute bangi na watumie unga." Kenga was not surprised that the fishermen assumed that they were rich kids playing truant. People had a perception that Asians were wealthy and Issa being one, it was automatically assumed that the two African kids with him were also rich.

Kenga kept his mind busy thinking about his sister without a leg. She would miss out on the swimming galas that she so much loved. The three had planned to go and see the gigantic carcass of the blue whale that had been washed ashore in the North Coast. This was an adventure for the following day, a Saturday. As he pondered over this, he felt Kadzo's hand in his and squeezed it. Obviously, he started, albeit softly, praying the *Tashbih*. He murmured the repentance *salah* thirty-three times under his breath.

The Good Samaritan driver had driven as fast as he could. Issa sat on the seat beside the driver. He was directing him to Wema

Nursing Home. He was so panic-stricken that at some point, he forgot to guide the driver. The two times he did this delayed the journey to the annoyance of Kenga and the driver. Issa's face turned red when Kadzo started to groan loudly. The driver had driven into Mpinzi Lane and lost the way to the nursing home. What his father would do to him when everything else was unearthed had tormented his mind and made him lose concentration.

At the Emergency Room, not much could be done apart from bandaging Kadzo's lower body. The clinical officer did what he could with the bandages and the painkillers they had but he could not help noticing that the boys looked stoned out of their minds. When he finished, he offered them an ambulance to rush Kadzo to the county hospital on the mainland.

Soon they were on the ferry across the channel. "*Mazee! Hii ni noma. Buda atazusha…*," Issa had kept murmuring incoherently over and over again. Twenty minutes later, Kadzo was in the Operating Theatre of Pwani Hospital where Issa's father worked. Kenga was saddled with the task of calling his parents. It was not easy telling them what had transpired but he summoned the courage to do it. His sister's life was in danger. She needed treatment; she needed blood transfusion and maybe an amputation.

* * *

A week had elapsed when Kenga went to the beach to thank the fishermen. When he looked at their favourite spot at the sea, there was something that made him happy after so many days of sadness and regrets. The same good Samaritans had managed to retrieve Safari Hatua from the high seas where it had drifted to.

As much as he had changed his mind on all the other activities he and his friends would engage themselves in, he cherished this small boat. His mood changed and his eyes shone.

"Maybe my sister's health would also be salvaged," he thought.

As he sat at the beach, he stared at the mighty coral wall that surrounded Fort Jesus. He imagined how the Portuguese possessed and controlled this place.

"Maybe Mono-eye, alias Big Man has taken us hostage," he narrowed his eyes for a better glimpse of the fort, "just like these white people had done with this beautiful fort. Now they are nowhere. They are gone." He threw his hands in the air. "Mmh! We can also flee. Flee from the attacks." He shifted his attention from this ancient archive of cannonballs and weapons of the lost war.

He looked at the tourists who were gathering around ready to enter the fort and made up his mind on what he wanted to do; to take up tour guiding over the weekend and stop drug peddling. Freedom milled his mind.

Chapter Five

A s soon as the seatbelt signal went off, Inspector Korir unbuckled, reclined his seat, closed his eyes and willed sleep. However, this was not possible, partly because he had been assigned the middle seat and the lady who sat on his right was like a parrot. She gave running commentaries on everyone and everything including the movie she was watching despite having her earphones on. He was not able to sleep. Countering the steady motion of his plan, his mind turned speedily, sifting through events of the preceding days and swirling them about in his brain. He tried to cue in to the normal sounds of the plane, the pressurised cabin, his right neighbour's constant chatter, the drifts of the other people's conversations from the next row and the clatter of the airhostess' trolleys being prepared for their passage up and down the aisle. He could not rest. His mind was pre-occupied with this current case. Being airborne, Korir had all the time in the world to think about this case. He wished the forty-five minutes flight to Mombasa would come to its planned end soon so that he could try and find out how his partner of barely one month had met his death.

The touchdown at Mombasa International Airport was uneventful. As the taxi approached the estate near the Kizingo waterfront where the police quarters were located, Inspector Korir noticed that nothing had changed since the last time he had come down here for a briefing with his partner. Hawkers were still competing for space on the crowded pavements; the potholes had tripled in size; the garbage dumped behind the flats where Sergeant Bilal had been housed had grown larger and the blocks of one-room apartments still begged for a fresh coat of paint but no one seemed to care. He hurriedly went up the stairs to the second floor, skipping two steps at a time, on a stairway that was originally painted white but was now brown in colour, with childish paintings courtesy of the many children sired by the cops. He was here to officially take over the apartment since Bilal had been murdered a few days earlier, in what the Chief Inspector said were unclear circumstances.

* * *

Inspector Korir was not yet thirty years old. He was one of the university graduates who had been incorporated into the police force several years ago to spruce up their image and make the force more professional. He had worked hard while training at the police academy and was full of enthusiasm and more often than not collided with the hardened attitudes of his older colleagues. Still, they respected him for his ingenuity in complex police investigations that had seen him rise up the ranks so fast. Korir had ended up in Mombasa after the Police Boss made a drastic reshuffle of senior police officers based in Mombasa and in the Anti-Narcotics Unit who were deemed to be complicit in the rampant drug trafficking.

When he had been transferred to the coastal city to tackle his current case, a strange fear had gripped him, just as it often happened to all first time visitors to Mombasa. Korir could not tell what exactly nauseated him but the culture of the coastal people had shocked him. Even those that had moved in from *bara* spoke and behaved like the native Waswahili. He had not taken time to walk the streets of this coastal city before but when he did, he wondered where he would start his assignment from and how he would speak to these people who seemed to speak a kind of Kiswahili he thought was so fine. Initially not happy about his transfer from the capital city, he had eventually become fond of the coastal port city.

Ever since he had been seconded to Mombasa to partner with Sergeant Bilal, Inspector Korir had been mesmerised by the pavement cafés of the Old Town. He was now addicted to the finger-licking dishes. His favourite was *kima chapati,* made of minced meat covered in a light oily dough, mixed with eggs and cooked on an open pan. Beside all the good life Mombasa was promising, he still wondered whether the assignment he had come here to do would ever bear fruits. He kept on looking at the people as they walked slowly on the streets and wondered whether they had the answers to his questions.

Chapter Six

Mr Karisa was alerted by the sound of strange voices. He heaved himself out of a deck service hatch that accessed the yacht he was repairing. His yard near the fort was becoming crowded and he needed to move to a bigger one but he loved working on the shores of the Indian Ocean with Fort Jesus as a backdrop. His tattered T-shirt and shorts were sodden with oil and there were lacerations on his arms and legs, where he had scratched himself on jagged metal as he repaired Mr Palmeri Macarroni's luxury yacht in the dim light. He just hoped that he did not contract tetanus or any other infection. If that happened, he would not afford to go to the hospital as he needed all the money he could get to pay for his daughter's hospital bill.

His fishing was not bringing in much money either. He supplemented his income by repairing yachts and boats of the rich expatriate community who had settled on the coastline. To make matters worse, his wife was sickly with diabetes and high blood pressure. Her condition had worsened, just as most of the things around him. She was in no position to help with the selling of fish at the local fish market.

He saw his son, Kenga, leading a tall slim man towards him. He left whatever he was doing to welcome his visitor as most

Africans do. He invited him to sit on the verandah of their Swahili house and after introductions, the talk continued.

"Mr Karisa, you must have had a feeling that something was wrong when your children started bringing in a lot of money," Inspector Korir said as he looked into Mr Karisa's eyes.

"No. Actually, I didn't, Inspector, because the expatriates around here are very generous to their bait boys and bait girls," Kadzo's father said as he avoided the inspector's gaze.

"It's only after the shark attack that I came to know that Kadzo and Kenga were working as drug couriers, using the speed boat I thought was a present from their Italian employer." Mr Karisa said as he wiped the oil that had spilled on his hand with the hem of his T-shirt. "That's when we also realised that they were using drugs."

Most people Korir had tried to interrogate had refused to talk candidly. They considered their silence as an act of courage and there was not much difference with Mr Karisa here.

"We shall see about that," the inspector said to himself wondering about Mr Karisa's naivety. It was a strange coincidence that the grown-ups did not bother to ask their kids where they got their expensive toys, such as Issa's Harley-Davidson motorbike. Korir wondered how parents did not even question their children when they sometimes became their families almost sole bread winners, like Kadzo and Kenga. It was the inspector's motto to always look for coincidences everywhere and in everything.

"So, is it okay if I go to the rehabilitation centre to talk to your daughter?" Korir leaned forward as if he did not want anyone else to know where he would be headed.

"I need help and she knows her way about the mainland and the drug lords' hangouts and meeting points. I need your permission to talk to her, Mr Karisa."

"I think that's okay. I don't see any problem if she's willing," Mr Karisa answered.

* * *

There were eight beds clustered in the tiny ward. The smallest ward at Pwani Hospital had been turned into a makeshift rehabilitation centre for drug addicts. None of the beds had pillows or bed sheets. As the breeze blew in from the ocean, the stench of excreta and disinfectant hit the inspector's nostrils. He did not give it much attention; his interest was in the young girl in the farthest corner bed. The inspector walked over to the girl and introduced himself.

"Hi Kadzo. My name is Inspector Korir. I'm really sorry about your leg but I'm glad you are alive. You're a very brave girl," the inspector said as he offered Kadzo his hand. Kadzo shook it, a little bit surprised because the cop looked so young.

"Thank you, Inspector."

After looking around, inspecting the other parts of the ward as most of his collegues in the discipline do, he came back to his subject.

"Kadzo, I've just talked to your father and he says that it's okay for you to talk to me," the inspector implored, emulating how the youth speak.

"I really need your help with a drug trafficking case I'm trying to crack," he said as he moved closer, as if he did not want anyone eavesdropping on the conversation.

"The investigations that my partner was about to conclude before he was murdered indicated that you know one of the drug barons," he paused and smiled at Kadzo as his eyes scanned her for any reaction, "and you've been dealing with him. One guy called Mustapha Jillo. That is until the shark attack," the inspector said without blinking, scrutinising Kadzo for any hint.

Kadzo's eyes widened and the inspector nodded.

"So what do you want to know? I've already made up my mind to stop peddling and using drugs. They are the reason I'm here."

"Bravo! That's very impressive. Why don't you start by telling me everything you know and how you met these guys." Inspector Korir knew that such reactions hinted victory on his part.

Before she could start talking to Inspector Korir, she pensively thought of the twenty thousand shillings a piece she and her brother would pocket whenever they ferried drugs for Big Man. She compared the value of money to that of her leg and then made a decision. She started talking.

"My brother and I are experts on any kind of speedboat. We had always followed our father out to sea whenever he went fishing," Kadzo started, as a smile curved on her lips. "That is how I ended up becoming a tomboy sort of," she said as she looked at her baggy T-shirt.

"In the past year, that experience came in handy because we knew every single inlet and twist of the entire Kenyan coastal strip.

Our parents are poor fisher folks who need any extra income that we can get." She looked down concealing the tears that were threatening to flow.

"All that they knew is that I was working as a bait girl for one of the rich Italian skippers while Kenga would occasionally help out as a bait boy," she said and shrugged.

"It doesn't hurt though, does it? Isn't it better than being a beach girl prostitute or my kid brother being a beach toy boy for those old foreign women?" She threw up her hands in self justification.

"Despite the fact that being the top girl in my class guarantees me a bursary from our constituency, that doesn't provide pocket money or sanitary pads for me. So isn't Big Man's quick and easy money better than spending a whole Saturday with *baba* from dawn to dusk, trying to fish, an exercise which rarely brings success?" Kadzo stared at the ground as if comparing her life before and after Mono-eye came into her life.

"Then along came Big Man. He's the boss," she adjusted herself in her bed and leaned on the wall. "Sometimes, we call him Mono-eye because he has a black cloth patch over his left eye, like the pirates we see in the movies," Kadzo giggled. "He never removes the eye patch though. One day, one of his stevedores told us that he lost his eye when he was fishing swordfish. The fish poked his eye," she said as she gestured.

"I've also never heard the stevedores call him Mustapha, maybe that is his real name but they call him Big Man," Kadzo continued as Korir nodded, gesturing her to go on.

"One day, Big Man came to me when I was fishing alone. My father had taken *mama* to the hospital and Kenga had gone for swimming practice at the school swimming pool. Big Man asked me to help him with a small business which could bring us extra income. I didn't refuse because we needed the money badly." Kadzo shrugged and closed her eyes as if reliving those moments. "At times, we could not even afford bus fare to school," she continued. "Normally, Big Man had freighters like the Somali type mother-ships, laden with more than three tonnes of cocaine. After working for him for a couple of months using one of my father's boats to ferry the cargo to various destinations, I realised that the cargo was always either cocaine or heroin but well disguised as 'innocent product,'" she said as she hit her hands to demonstrate the quantity of the product.

"Big Man is the one who bought us our speedboat, Safari Hatua. He said that *baba's* dhows were too slow for the job. The ships carrying the cargo would anchor in Kenya's territorial waters for more than half a month and the local and international drug traffickers would purchase the drugs during this time. The freighter that had frequently brought tonnes of cargo was blown up on the day of the shark attack. The explosion might have blown the lid off these operations as well," Kadzo told Korir wishing that her last words would discourage the cop from asking more questions or daring to catch up with Mono-eye, who without doubt, seemed to be a dangerous man. Against Kadzo's wishes, Korir seemed to want more information. He nodded and signaled her to continue.

"Among the buyers Kenga and I have encountered aboard the mother-ships are African drug barons, some linked to piracy and international terrorism and a couple of Mombasa-based businessmen." Kadzo pulled a handkerchief from under her pillow and wiped her eyes. Korir wondered whether she felt sad for her involvement in the business or tears formed in her eyes because of the loss of her leg. He empathised with her and encouraged her to speak.

"When you speak out things get well for you and the other youth," Korir encouraged her.

"We always used Safari Hatua to ferry the drugs from the ships which mostly sailed in from different countries to various Kenyan coastal beaches. We were ever busy; Big Man gave us big jobs at least twice every month because of our knowledge of the coastline." Korir was awed by the girl's confession. He wanted to know the times of the month when bigger consignments would be brought in but thought otherwise. He gestured Kadzo to go on.

"We knew every nook and cranny of the waters to the extent that we could not hit barrier reefs even if we sailed with our eyes closed. We would drop the cargo at points along River Galana, Kinango, Malindi, Kilifi, Mtwapa, Formosa Bay, Kipini, Lamu, Patta Island and Chambone among others," Kadzo explained as she counted all these places with her fingers.

The inspector motioned her to continue as he felt the girl still owed him a lot of information.

"I think the blast was as a result of differences between the drugs kingpin and the ship owners following a change of plans on who they should hand over the cocaine to. Mono-eye might have ordered the drugs using a different name or person altogether,"

Kadzo said in a tone suggesting that Big Man was capable of both her guesses.

"Before the blast, we had transported several tonnes to Kinango and Mtwapa creeks using Safari Hatua. I had a feeling that Big Man was telling his henchmen to kill us because we had tried to tell him what our plans were," she paused as she tried to recall the events that preceded the shark attack.

"We didn't want to continue acting as couriers for him," Kadzo stared at the floor reliving the nasty experience.

"I remember very well how one of the stevedores received the gesture from Big Man," she repeated the gesture Big Man had given the stevedoves on the day of the shark attack. "He lunged at me and fortunately or unfortunately, the blast occurred then preventing him from doing what he had been commanded to do as he scampered for safety. We were thrown into the ocean," Kadzo said throwing her hands in the air, "and that is how I was attacked by the shark. Maybe the blast was God-sent as Mono-eye might have wanted us killed."

Inspector Korir listened attentively, jotting a few notes in his green note book.

"It might shock you that this trade goes on for months in Kenya's territorial waters without raising suspicions or arrests being made." Kadzo shook her head as if what she was saying sounded mysterious even to her, "We saw cops come aboard the freighters on speedboats and leave with thousands of dollars as payback. We never feared when the police approached or boarded our boat because we knew they were friends of the barons, or so we thought."

This statement drew a frown from Inspector Korir. He cleared his throat as if to speak but did not. He just gestured Kadzo to continue, a thin layer of sweat forming on his face.

"We have to admit that our country has been turned into a playground for international drug traffickers. The drug trade in the country is facilitated by security personnel and top politicians." Kadzo indicated with her hand, a gesture that Korir interpretted to mean 'their relatives and friends'. "This is what I know. It is hard to get out once you become a peddler like Kenga, Issa and I," she shook her head and wiped a tear.

It was obvious that she regretted her partnership with Mono-eye. "The pay is more than most professions can offer." Kadzo shuddered as she said this. She tried to imagine how she and her family would live now that she did not have a leg and her determination to stop working for Big Man was strong.

She still had more information for Korir and so, she continued. "We started using drugs because everyone on the ships was doing so. We also needed more courage to handle the 'powder' that cost so much and which everybody sought." Kadzo shuddred again as if not using drugs while peddling them was more life threatening.

"These drug traffickers are licensed to carry firearms and when you don't snort cocaine with them, they might as well shoot you," she said with desperation. Korir could see how the teenagers had felt that they had no choice, especially Kadzo and Kenga. He saw that their need for money had driven them into drug peddling. He asked Kadzo whether she still wanted to speak out.

"I have no problem Inspector; I will tell you everything I know," Kadzo assured him.

"Kambo was shot because he had joined the team so as to earn money to pay for his education and not get involved. Mono-eye could not trust him."

"'That can't be!' Mono-eye had told the stevedoves. 'I want that dirt cleaned,' he had declared angrily. The poor orphan boy was buried with his dreams just when he was about to sit his high school examinations." Kadzo buried her face in her hands for a few seconds before she could speak again. "We feared for our lives when this happened and gave in to the habit. Soon, we graduated from acting as couriers and started peddling cocaine and heroin in our neighbourhoods and at school," Kadzo said as she curved her shoulders. "We also sold some to addicts at the Shimanzi godowns in Industrial Area, which have become notorious drug peddler's dens. This was more lucrative because we were sure of earning money on a daily basis. We got a lot of money and gave it to *baba* for *mama's* medication."

Kadzo raised her face as if she was through and then said in finality, "To save them a lot of agony, we told our parents that we were working as bait girl and bait boy for an Italian expatriate. We also convinced them that he was the one who had given us Safari Hatua as a present."

Inspector Korir could not believe that teenagers of that age had succeeded in concealing their act so successfully. "This is a totally different century," he told himself.

"Our parents might have started suspecting that we had lied but by then, it was already too late; we were fully in the business." Korir looked at Kadzo and saw her helplessness. It was obvious that the girl's intentions were clear: to earn some income. He also noted that taking some drugs would help them do their business without causing suspicion.

"I have been at the top of my class at school and my parents have never given me or my brother any pocket money. Not that they refuse but they don't have enough to spare. So I have to find my own ways of getting some. There you have my story, Inspector." She stared on the wall of the ward and the inspector could not tell whether she regretted or felt satisfication for having given Mono-eye away.

She turned and looked at Inspector Korir. She wanted to know what his reaction was. Did he have this 'you are also guilty' attitude? The inspector sighed. His face did not reveal any feelings. He just sighed.

"So will you help me with my plan, Kadzo? If you want to truly reform, will you help me nab Big Man?" Inspector Korir asked.

"You bet I'm in!" Kadzo quipped back.

Chapter Seven

Inspector Korir's heart was beating a little faster. The palpitations were almost overwhelming and he knew why. After his lengthy talk with Kadzo, it was now clear that he was up against the same Mustapha Jillo alias Big Man who had jumped bail some years back. Soon, his mind was trapped in Big Man's offer he had turned down a few years back.

"Should I have let him go that one time and then later linked up with him for a hefty payback? How did I benefit when Big Man was freed on bond and is as free as a bird out there? He is now a drug baron. Maybe I will end up in the hands of this merciless criminal," the inspector thought as he stood at the window of his office and looked out at the blue ocean in the horizon.

The sorrow of how many cops came aboard with an enthusiastic idealism, which was soon replaced with a definite eye for a fat bank balance crowded him. He tried to control his fluttering heart and thought of the day his partner had been murdered.

That morning, the Chief Inspector had appeared indignant and angry that someone had dared shoot and kill one of his cops. His hackles had been up and his nerves raw. But now, Inspector Korir was beginning to have misgivings about his boss. For the drug traffickers and barons to reign in this coastal paradise, senior police officers had to be in their payrolls.

"The report coming in is that Sergeant Bilal has been killed."

The chilling words had come from the Chief Inspector.

"A shooting in broad daylight as he drove in his car. Nothing was stolen."

Press coverage of Sergeant Bilal's murder was on all television and radio channels at prime time news. A cop considered too nosy had simply been gunned down! The fact that Bilal was not yet married and so had no children was a little consoling but he had parents and siblings who were grieving. Korir had barely spent a couple of weeks with his colleague. He remembered how a few days earlier, the government advisor report had said that drug lords and money launders were possible financiers of terrorist activities in the region. He had expressed his fear that the steady flow of drugs money would be used to stimulate other criminal activities if the vice was not tamed. Korir decided to sit down and read the dossier put together by Bilal before he had been shot dead.

He read the hundred-page dossier and jotted down the most important points in his green notebook. Every point in Bilal's report indicated why he had to be exterminated. If this information ever reached the media, so many functions of the government would stall as the holders of these offices would be in prison with no judge or magistrate to judge them! This would give the journalist a shouting headline *Death of the Government*. No, they would not allow Bilal to push the government to the wall. Korir shook his head and shuddered. He was amazed at the intricacy of the syndicate; those at the top benefiting from the trade financially while the larger base – addicts, are losing their lives every passing second. Korir was glad that Kadzo and Kenga had pulled themselves out of the snare. He wished that many other younger people would emulate the two.

Korir finally understood why the recent *utafiti* report had indicated that Kenya and the Eastern African region had become new routes for traffickers following tighter controls in the countries known to be drug trafficking hubs. The heroin or cocaine that was brought in from Asian countries was usually taken to bonded warehouses and repackaged before it was redistributed to local and regional dealers.

As Korir closed the file, the thought of the recent blast aboard Big Man's Italian investor friend's freighter and the subsequent shark attack on Kadzo, clouded his mind. Poverty had forced that girl into being a courier for the barons on the fishing sites and now her leg was amputated. He decided to work with this girl and her brother. This way, he would find out how easy it had become to ferry the white powder from the high seas. He sat at his desk for a long while, pensively thinking of what a tough battle this was to fight! To break the tension that was building up in his nerves, he decided to read a newspaper that had been on his table unattended for weeks.

"Freighter valued at 100 million destroyed in mysterious blast. The ship, belonging to an Italian investor, caught fire at Shimoni Creek in Kwale County. On being contacted, the owner said that the ship drifted from where it was anchored while they were in the deep-sea fishing and hit an electric cable at Club Marine before exploding into a huge fireball. A potential witness, a young girl who it appears was aboard the ship and a champion swimmer was thrown overboard – she was attacked by a shark and lost a leg. She is now recuperating at the Pwani Hospital, where she underwent surgery."

Korir's mind was already at work. My colleagues think that the freighter's blowing up was as a result of a spark on a leaky fuel engine but I think otherwise. I think it was a blackmail gone wrong and I intend to prove my suspicions right.

Chapter Eight

Issa turned into a side alley and stopped. He glanced around severally before opening the heavy doors of the abandoned mosque located in Bondeni on the fringes of the Old Town's sea wall. The mosque was silent as it was not yet time for the *adhuhuri* prayers. He went into a backroom and made his way into the dark silence. He moved to the furthest shadowy corner and sat down beside a black curtain.

Inspector Korir went to the back of the mosque and eavesdropped from an open window. After a moment, he heard Issa call hesitantly, "Mr Big Man!"

A deep voice from behind the curtain said, "Good evening, Issa. I don't have a lot of time. Are you ready for business? You also have to go to the airport for your weekly errand."

They started whispering and Korir had to strain to listen. He gave up and waited for Issa to leave.

A short while later, Issa walked out of the mosque stuffing a small parcel into the back pocket of his jeans and walked into the cool evening. Inspector Korir followed him as he strolled to the market. He stood at a stall to eat ripe bananas as he watched the lad buy some cauliflowers, vermicelli and garlic onions from an old woman whom he chatted with heartily. The old lady put the vegetables into a plastic bag before handing them to the boy. Issa then crossed the busy Digo Road and sat down at Mubin's Pavement Café. He removed the small parcel from his pocket and put it into the bottom of the vegetable bag.

He then walked back to the vegetable vendor and gave her the bag of vegetables. He told her that he had to go somewhere else before taking the vegetables to his mother. He promised to come back later for his vegetables. That was when it hit Inspector Korir that a transaction had already taken place! It seemed that Issa was the only one of the trio who was unrepentant and continued to peddle drugs.

Issa then flagged down a taxi. Korir did not want to lose the fish on his bait. He got into his borrowed BMW and followed the taxi, cruising slowly lest Issa suspected that he was being followed.

They were driving out of town and were soon in the direction of the north-west side of Mombasa Island. As they drove over the Kibarani flyover and towards the airport, the cool breeze from the Makupa Causeway alleviated, albeit only a little bit, the humid coastal heat. Korir wondered where they were headed. He hoped that his effort would lead to greater discoveries. He feared losing Issa; so he kept his eyes on the red Peugeot taxi.

* * *

Korir was surprised when the taxi driver paid the entrance fee into the airport. He followed suit, not knowing what to expect or do once inside the airport. In the parking lot, Issa seemed to tell the driver to wait for him. He left the taxi driver and walked into the arrivals section of the airport. Korir parked his BMW a few slots from the taxi and followed Issa.

Issa went and sat near the waving bay on level one. Korir followed him and sat a short distance away, and flipped through a magazine he had bought in the lounge shop. Half an hour later, the arrival of the India flight was announced. Korir watched as the passengers that had disembarked went through immigration.

"Mr Issa Abdul, passenger from India. Please, go to the lost luggage office on level two," the airport speakers came on with the message, after a short while, Inspector Korir followed Issa at a distance. He watched from afar, amazed, as Issa was not asked for any identification by the airport official in charge.

"Yours, I believe Sir, which was lost in transit as you reported. It has finally turned up as we told you it would," the official spoke to Issa cheerfully as he handed him a small black trolley bag.

Korir whistled softly to himself in amazement. He knew that the suitcase contained cocaine disguised in one form or another. Korir was sure that the officials had not checked the bag. He had to bid his time. He could not just walk up to Issa and say, "Contrary to Section 4 (a) of the Narcotics Drugs and Psychotropic Substances Control Act of 1994, I hereby arrest you for drug trafficking." No! the drug barons' ground network was intricate and this young man was sooner rather than later going to get into big trouble. It was not the time to confront him. Korir kept wondering why Issa, who seemed to come from a well off family, trafficked drugs. Was it just for the thrill of it? Korir came to the conclusion that the bag had been put aboard the plane with no passenger but arrangements had been made for Issa to pick it up at the airport. It seemed this was a weekly schedule, judging from Big Man's earlier words. Korir watched the young man as he went outside and got into the waiting taxi which sped off.

Chapter Nine

"**K**adzo my dear, you are only seventeen and your brother is sixteen. He's younger and you should be setting a better example for him. I'm glad that you've both stopped peddling and using drugs." Kadzo looked at Mrs Christine, their English teacher, who doubled as the school's guidance counsellor. She dropped her eyes.

"I promise to do my best, Mrs Christine. It's just that the nightmares have been horrendous. Sometimes, I have nobody to talk to. It's not as if there are shark attack victims on every street corner."

"You can always come and talk to me," she said reasuringly. "You shouldn't spoil your good grades now that you'll be in Form Four next year. I want you to be at the top in this county, if not in the whole country," Mrs Christine said as she moved closer and placed her right hand on Kadzo's shoulder.

"You should begin by first getting out of your pity party now that at the moment, you can't compete in the swimming gala as you get used to your new leg. There is something that can keep you busy," she smiled broadly and continued.

"Why not enter the national essay writing contest organised by the anti-narcotics agency?" Mrs Christine offered confidently as if she knew that Kadzo would excel in such an activity. "I understand that you've also initiated an income generating project? Tell me about that," she enquired as she looked at Kadzo and placed her hand in hers.

"Well, I just thought that since I've now stopped peddling drugs and acting as a courier for that drug baron, I should make some money in some other way. This is because we need the money at home for our mother's medications. We also need some pocket money," Kadzo said with confidence. Mrs Christine could feel the determination in the girl's voice. "I know many teenagers who are good at riding speedboats and who are familiar with our coastal line and tourist attractions. I have set up a group of us who will be acting as tour guides over the weekends and on school holidays." She looked at Mrs Christine as if asking for advice but it appeared as if the teacher was so impressed with her initiative that she signaled her to tell her more.

"I am also initiating a sort of rehabilitation centre where we shall counsel other teens and help them come out of the habit that almost saw me get killed."

Mrs Christine eagerly prodded Kadzo to tell her more as she was keen that the girl did not relapse to her old habits.

* * *

Very early the following morning before classes began, Kadzo lifted her satchel bag from her locker, hesitated and put it back inside. She picked up the foolscap on which she had written her essay and scrutinised it carefully. Dare she hand it in? She sighed and tossed the paper aside just as Kenga burst into the classroom.

"Sis! Guess what?" Kenga said excitedly as he rushed towards his sister.

"From the look on your face, I'd say that your timing in freestyle has just beaten the world record!"

"No! Guess again."

"You've gotten straight As in all your subjects."

"Close."

"Well?"

"I got an A in math!"

"Pinch me," Kadzo said, "Pinch me hard and wake me up."

"It's true," Kenga gloated.

"How on earth did that miracle happen?"

"I've been working hard – I just thought that with all the grief we've caused our parents lately, its time I repented. You should also repent. You know you scared Mother with your shark attack!" Kenga scolded his elder sister.

"Yeah. You're right," Kadzo repeatedly muttered, "I'm the one in trouble because I got you into this. The police will send me to prison. Father and Mother will blame me for everything."

"Nobody will send you or me to prison, Sister. Not if we tell the same truth and help Inspector Korir with his investigations. The police will have to believe us. Actually, come to think of it – let us just stick to the truth that we desperately needed the money. Now I've got to rush for the swimming practice!" Kenga said.

As she watched her brother's retreating back, a rush of guilt swept over her. She had caused so many problems recently. If Kenga was already making amends, maybe she should throw her doubts out of the window and hand in her essay to Mrs Christine for the essay writing competition.

***

When the bell for recess rang a couple of days later, Kadzo left her class. They still had the last lesson of the day, physics. She limped quickly through the hallway of the science laboratories and out of the front door into the sunlight. Students hurried in every direction in groups, talking, giggling and walking towards the cafeteria. Kadzo avoided the direction of the cafeteria as if it was a plague. She quickened her step, pulling herself with baby steps. Her mind was busy sketching the rest of the day.

She had a lot to do, but her priority number one was polishing her essay's second draft. They had all gotten feedback on their individual pieces from Mrs Christine.

She spent part of the half hour recess basking in the sunlight on a bench. The sun rays relieved the ache in her healing leg. The most difficult part of her day was walking in her artificial leg to the third floor. She had to climb the stairs as that was where her classroom was located. What was she supposed to do? Request the principal to move their class to the ground floor when it had been her fault that she lost her leg?

"Please, hallway, stay empty," Kadzo whispered as she steadily clumped up the stairs. Several classroom doors were open to let in the breeze; Kadzo did not want any of the students to start staring outside at the clumsy person thumping up the stairs.

When she reached the door of Form 3A, she listened closely for signs that someone would be coming now that recess had ended and maybe push her to the floor. But all was quiet. She heard no conversation, footsteps nor laughter. Strains of music coming across from the music room on the opposite landing indicated that the music group was seriously practising for the upcoming inter-county competitions. She had made it up safely. Lately, she had made a habit of coming to school very early in the morning and was usually the last to leave. She did this so that the other students would not notice the clumsiness of her new leg.

Chapter Ten

The Coastal Ports Agency dockyard looked incredible. Inspector Korir had never seen so many vehicles in one place before. Thousands of them and of all makes glinted in the sunlight from their vantage point up on the road. It had been two agonising months of waiting for Kadzo to get well so that she could help him with his investigations. Kenga was too busy with his swimming practice for the upcoming gala and Issa did not seem interested in helping.

This particular day, Kadzo had showed him the house in the Old Town where they sometimes met with Big Man to receive instructions. They had decided to follow two stevedores who had been there alone. There were cranes all around lifting hundreds of containers full of cars and other goods from ships which had docked in the port. Hundreds of casual labourers carried gunny bags of produce, mainly cereals.

"But the beamers man!" Korir stared down at the cars again.

"Stop staring, Inspector," Kadzo rebuked. "Stranger than fiction things happen here, stowaways ... smuggling of drugs ... thefts of containers ... deaths ... you may even find a cache of firearms hidden in one of these cars."

Korir stared at her dumbfounded but before he could say anything, they were approached by the two men they had followed! One of them was of Arab descent dressed in a black and white T-shirt branded with a skull and bones emblem. The other one was an African with a blue and white bandana tied around his head.

"Excuse me," the Arab said, "we saw you two down at the house near the Old Town snooping around and now you've followed us here," the man said as he stared at the two with a wild sneer on his face.

"Young girl, you don't seem to have learnt a lesson from the shark attack. If you know what is good for you, *afadhali muishie*," he warned them off in Swahili slang.

"You must have heard of accidental deaths where someone has been crushed by a container and investigations never concluded," he threatened, while his *miraa* chewing friend kept quiet, holding a penknife. Its blade glinting suggestively in the fierce sunlight.

They then walked away nonchalantly and entered the grey metallic Toyota Rav4 they had been driving.

"Look at that baby!" Korir whistled.

"You can get one here at the port if you talk nicely to someone, for as low as fifty thousand shillings," Kadzo told him in a veiled way alluding to the rampant corruption that bedeviled the port.

"But you have to act very fast because people have woken up on a day when the public auction is scheduled only to find all the cars gone! *Ati* they've been bought or cleared – overnight!" she giggled.

"Come on!" Korir urged, "Let's follow these guys. They're driving off."

Kadzo got into Korir's car and he drove very fast. This time, he made sure that the occupants of the Rav4 did not suspect that they were being followed again! They went down the Port Road, but soon diverted to Haile Selassie Avenue and branched into Kenyatta Avenue. They drove through some dingy alley streets. Korir realised they had driven into Majengo when he saw the Swahili houses. He had been here before and so he knew it was a Swahili estate.

The youth loitering in the neighbourhood looked stoned. They were chewing khat while staring absent-mindedly into space, hardly noticing Kadzo and Korir approach as they followed the other car. Korir slowed down when he saw the grey Rav 4 pull over near one dilapidated verandah. He did the same and parked in a manner that his car was partly hidden by the wing of an extension protruding from a house.

This part of the neighbourhood looked deserted. They saw the two men enter a house that looked almost rundown. Korir and Kadzo got out of the car and peered into the house over one window that was partly closed. Korir saw the men sit down. They were talking to a man who was hidden in the shadows. He ducked when one of the men glanced towards the window. Kadzo could not see properly but at least, she got snippets of the conversation.

"Did you manage to warn that snooping inspector and the now crippled girl?" the shadowy figure asked.

"Yes, Sir," one of the men replied.

"If this inspector insists on investigating our operations, he'll end up just like his buddy. I think we'll have no more cargo runs for a while," the hidden figure added.

"Why?" the khat chewing stevedore interjected.

"You are asking why? Haven't you been listening to what these government dudes have been promising *wananchi*? That a new anti-narcotics unit has been set up. You can bet it's going to be tight running any operations for a while!"

At that moment two middle aged European men came from the inner recesses of an adjacent chamber. They were talking rapidly in Italian. Issa followed them.

"Oh my!" Kadzo exclaimed. "It's Issa! So you were right – he's not stopped peddling and yet he promised his parents that he was going to stop."

The Italians sat down making consultations with the shadowy figure in low tones. They kept referring to him as Mustapha.

The shadowy figure formed a steeple with his fingers and rubbed his chin thoughtfully, his elbows resting on the table.

"Mmh ... this new political dispensation ... mmh ... the scenario looks appetising though... Let us see how the devolution works out and then we can touch base in our usual way, with the new power brokers or alternatively, form a few new fronts or off-shore investments to help us out of these tax evasion claims by the revenue authorities."

As if being controllled from a central point, they stood up and walked towards the rear door.

"I think the earlier we start the better ... this guy at the immigration ... what is his name?" the shadowy figure continued talking as they disappeared into the back door.

"... Wanyeki, I think...," one of the Italians replied.

"...what about the charter licence? Have you talked properly to anyone at the directorate of civil aviation?"

A door banged and suddenly, Korir and Kadzo heard simultaneous roars of three powerful cars in the opposite direction.

"Shit!" Korir said disgustingly as he hit the bonnet of the Rav4 that was still parked outside the door. "How on earth did they do that?"

"We've lost them. Sorry. I should have warned you when they stood up. Swahili houses have remained stuck in a time warp, in their very own architectural designs. They are always built with a back door," Kadzo explained.

"I can understand that their boss and the Italians are so careful. The clever dudes have backtracked and driven off! The stevedores must have double-parked another car behind there!" Korir cursed.

"But at least I think we've hit pay dirt!" he continued. "We can take down the registration number of this 'baby' and you can use your journalist-in-training nose to help us out. We can get someone at the registrar of motor vehicles to run a check on these plates. I'm sure this is a bull's eye!" Korir looked pleased as he whipped out his note book and pen.

"Come on. Let's go home. I'll treat you to one of your coastal delicacies. What shall you teach me to savor today?" he asked Kadzo as he pulled her off the kerb where she had sat down dejected.

Chapter Eleven

Feeling Kadzo tugging on his arm, Inspector Korir stared at the chef outside Mubin's Café, deftly flipping a chapatti in his pan. The Inspector's mouth started to water. He laughed self-consciously.

"Alright kids, where shall we try out today?" he asked Kadzo and Kenga, who had joined them.

"Why don't we try Sharrif's Delight? It's further up the street. Their Shish kebabs are simply fantastic," Kadzo answered.

They walked along Kisauni Street. This street was ever crowded in the evening. The locals usually came out at this time and gathered in *barazas*, to chat and gossip. Others just came out to sample the delicacies, in what had become a ritual to them.

Later, the policeman gave the kids a lift and dropped by their house to say hello to their mother and check on how she was doing. Korir was simply amazed at the co-existence in this county of different religions. The Muslims lived in the same neighbourhood with Christian and Hindu friends with no problem at all. He found the kids' mother squatting on a *mbuzi* grating coconuts. She chatted with them happily. When they eventually entered the house, she stood up to serve them lunch. Korir was glad that the medication was bringing Mrs Karisa back to life.

After the meal, he signaled Kenga and Kadzo and they followed him outside to the narrow alley.

"So. What next?" asked Kenga.

"I think we should learn to fight this drug menace together, as a community," Korir replied.

"How?" Kadzo countered. "Do you think other people have not tried? These drugs are available on every street corner. Everywhere you turn," she said as she turned to look around, "kids are talking of shooting up with syringes and most of them are dying of overdoses. We've heard of some who faint after having their first shots of heroin, only to slip into a coma and never to wake up!" her voice rose and the motion of her hands indicated desperation.

"We've stopped peddling but there are still thousands of peddlers surrounding us!" Kadzo shook her head resignedly.

"Come. Let me show you how easy it is," Kadzo told Korir.

She approached a young boy who looked unkempt. "*Leo haunipambi?*" Kadzo asked him in Swahili slang.

He silently shook his head and walked away.

Korir wondered aloud how Kadzo knew that the guy was a peddler. "Don't get surprised. We can pick them out very easily. They leave a bandana hanging out of their back pockets in a certain way," Kenga answered him. Korir was stunned.

"Huyu sueba wako ni mwera?" another stoned youth who looked like a zombie approached and asked Kenga.

"Zii!" Kenga denied emphatically in the same language.

After several attempts, Korir got the eerie feeling that the community was closing ranks, sort of protecting their own.

Emaciated youth who were hard hit pretended to play a board game while others played *dumna,* a game that is almost like dominoes. They seemed to avoid Kenga, Kadzo and Korir's eyes.

Korir sensed that it was difficult that day for the two kids to get any supply because they had come with a stranger who was most probably letting off unmistakable vibes that he was a cop – maybe in his stance and walk. Korir realised they were going to make no headway. He made a hands out signal to the kids, the way referees do in basketball or football and added with a silent nod. They were to leave.

Chapter Twelve

A day later, the streets of Mombasa were filled with the young and the old. Kadzo and some community members had organised a peaceful demonstration against drug abuse and trafficking. They marched through the Old Town and ended up at the main police post where they were addressed by the anti-narcotics police boss. Inspector Korir was simply fascinated as he followed the crowd along the narrow alleys of the town. He had been told by Kadzo that some anti-narcotics crusaders and sympathisers would be joining the protest march.

The Old Town architecture was amazing. Korir wanted to reach out and touch the ornate carved wooden doors with designs copied from ancient Portuguese dhows but he controlled this urge. The narrow lanes were full of people and wares. There was a bustle of activities with a magnetic pulse of its very own. He was almost oblivious of the chants of the crowd who carried placards and banners bearing protest slogans. They waved them in the air magnificently as they passed the Indian shops opposite the Mackinnon Market.

The numerous hawkers made the alleys look even tinier and the placards with all manner of colours magnified the purpose of the peaceful demonstration. Inspector Korir, Kadzo and Kenga pushed and shoved as they followed the crowd of demonstrators towards the main police post. The demonstrators mingled with shoppers causing some of them to change their mind and join the crusaders. The idling young people found themselves demonstrating against what kept them high. Kenga and Kadzo knew them and they hoped that they changed for the better.

Inspector Korir was startled by a loud voice that boomed and swallowed the other voices. It was the Muezzin calling for noon prayers. The faithful started closing shops hurriedly and soon all those who were interested in the business of eradicating drug abuse and trafficking filled the streets and the shop verandahs. The crowd trekked through the old buildings on Kibokoni Road; braving a twist, another turn and more ancient buildings, glazed windows, empty shutters, a trellis on a verandah, balconies supported by wooden brackets, aged wooden columns still standing firm, ancient architecture that still holds your eye … such finesse.

"Why was it now a den of cocaine and heroin?" Korir wondered. "Why had this beautiful Old Town been let to go to the dogs and cause such trauma among the young and the old?"

The silence on this drug issue was deafening. Who knew what secrets, what family tears were hidden in this foreboding silence with only the shutters creaking on hinges almost falling off? It had to take the deaths of several youth and accidents like the loss of Kadzo's leg for this demonstration to take place.

The hot noon sun passed over into the afternoon. By now, the crowd had swelled with curious onlookers streaming in. They had neared the sea wall and water was trickling down some open drainage system into the Indian Ocean. The crowd swelled into the public stadium overlooking the old harbour. Korir forgot about the crowd for a while as he stared across the customs buildings where a dhow was preparing to leave for Somalia. It was laden with sugar and other exports.

"Are the dhows docking there inspected for drugs?" he jotted down in his notebook to follow that up.

The sound of the sea was very near; the huge Fort Jesus looked imposing. Korir imagined how it had looked in the sixteenth century with the Portuguese barricading themselves from other invaders. He had been on the other side of this fort and seen so many dhows in the shallow waters facing a prestigious residential estate. He could not tell what the small dhows carried but he had been gripped by an eerie feeling. The city was so beautiful but he wondered what the people did with the beauty.

Suddenly, Kadzo jerked him back to consciousness as they took the long stretch of road to the police post. The large crowd of demonstrators formed a picket in front of the main police post. They were shouting and asking for the city police boss. A few junior police officers came out to try and calm the rowdy mob but they did not prevail. The crowd continued chanting, clapping and stumping. Eventually, the boss came out to address the crowd. They shouted at him. The elderly parents of children from the Old Town especially did not give him a chance to be heard.

"Tafadhali nisikilizeni!" he implored.

"Sisi tumechoka Bwana! Watoto wetu wamekuwa waizi kwa sababu hawana pesa za kununua unga. Unga kama ukucha ni shillingi mia mbili. Wasichana wanakuwa malaya na wavuluna mashoga ili tu wapate ndong'a," one agitated old man shouted. *"Kila kitu kilikuwa ni mwiko! Mwiko! Mwiko! Kuzungumza na watoto juu ya kufanya mapenzi ni mwiko! Hiki kimya kimezidi! Kuzungumzia juu ya ukimwi ilikuwa ni mwiko; sasa huu ugonjwa umewaua jamii zetu. Sasa pia kuzungumza juu ya madawa ya kulevya ni mwiko?"*

"Jameni! watoto wamezubaa hawa! Hili ni janga kuu!" a woman screamed from the crowd.

"Hii maneno itaangaliwa," the officer kept insisting.

"Hatutaki hizo ahadi za bure! Tumechoka! Wauzaji mnawashika; mahakamani wanaachiliwa! Mbona hamwakamatii mababe wenye kuleta madawa nchini? Na wenye kuwalipa vijana wauze huu unga?"

Some women took hold of Kadzo and brought her to the front where the police boss was standing. One old woman addressed him as she held Kadzo's hand.

"Huyu msichana shupavu ndiye anayeongoza maandamano haya. Unaona alipoteza mguu baharani kwa papa akijihusisha na madawa ya kulevya? Lakini amewacha anataka kuwasaidia wenzake! Wewe utafanya nini kumaliza jinamizi hili la ndonga?"

Korir was taking down a few notes from the vantage point where the local media and news crew had positioned themselves.

A few people turned violent and threw stones at the Police Post. The crowd refused to be dispersed and anti-riot police had to be called in to disperse them. Tear gas canisters flew everywhere. Korir found himself holding Kadzo's hand and running for their lives as their eyes watered. They were lucky because Kadzo had had her artificial leg fixed afresh. It enabled her to run a bit faster to a safe place! From a distance, they watched as a lorry with the chemically treated water meant to sting rioters screeched to a halt. Everybody scattered in different directions.

Chapter Thirteen

Shimoni! Korir could not believe that he was reliving the history lessons he had learnt as a teenager in high school. These were the historic caves! Kadzo reflected on the last time they were supposed to be here. It was here they were to deliver the cargo on the day of the shark attack. The explosion aboard Big Man's freighter that fateful day had changed all that. They were now covering the last 14 km down a sandy road just after Ramisi on the Mombasa-Lunga Lunga Road. After a while, they were finally there. To the kids, it was odd paying the entrance fee to get into the caves. They were used to coming in through the channel to hide the cargo.

As they guided Inspector Korir and his colleague, Corporal Mwangi who had accompanied him to the caves, Kadzo was kicking herself mentally. Why had she told these officers anything about this place? She was scared to be back here. She was now pointing the way into the caves but her nerves were stiff. The Shimoni Caves were a favourite hideout for most drug traffickers. They sometimes came to this place to get a boat to Wasini Island. Kadzo remembered the number of times Mono-eye had treated them to a sumptuous lunch at Betty's Camp across the road. She feared that he would be there. She was not prepared for a confrontation with Big Man himself; it was only his trade she was determined to terminate.

Inspector Korir stared at the entrance dubiously. He walked around the boulders and examined the slippery corals on all sides. "Let's take a look inside," he finally said as if against his better instincts.

In the main cave, the first thing that was illuminated by the beam from Inspector's electric torch were the chains used by the *wazungus* to keep the slaves captive. These rusted iron rings were believed to have been used to hold slaves captive before being shipped to the main slave market in Zanzibar where they worked on spice plantations before being shipped abroad. This sight took him back to his history classes again but this was not his business at the moment. It was just a path to the truth. To him, these chains of slavery were still so strong in the coastal city and the country as a whole. The only difference was the destination of the two categories of slaves. Korir was again transferred to his own world as the kids prompted him to concentrate on the task.

Kenga led his sister, Korir and his colleague to where he had anchored Safari Hatua after picking it from the fishermen who had retrieved the boat from the high seas after the shark attack. They had to use the speedboat now to cross the channel and show Big Man's other hideouts to the cops. As the twin-turbo speedboat scudded north towards Diani, Kenga let Kadzo have the wheel.

She sat low on the rear passenger banquette, both hands gripping the bolster seat in front of her. The sleek-nosed vessel hung in mid-air as its hull skimmed another swell. After what seemed like an eternity, it crashed down into the water again, sending walls of white spray high up into the sky. The two cops watched her in admiration as she took over the wheel and handled the powerful boat expertly through the swells. She knew the treacherous reefs and the sandbars like the back of her hand and could navigate the coastline at night or even while blindfolded. She eased forward Safari Hatua's throttles and brought the boat around in a gentle arc so that the thin strip of beach on the horizon was now off the starboard bow.

The detectives observed the clean line of the wake and were impressed. The girl certainly knew how to pilot her boat. Soon the engine note changed as she throttled back. They had reached their destination. Ahead was the untidy mouth of Marine Creek on River Kinango; the muddy river current was staining the blue ocean at a point where the river met the ocean. Kadzo steered and swept the boat in a shallow arc into the navigation channel. A second speedboat came into view with low-lung lines. The black-painted fountain boat which had turned into the creek now made a rapid erratic progress along the ocean line towards the inlet.

There were several men in the boat. All of them were wearing black leather jackets and baseball caps.

"Get down!" the Corporal shouted. It was when Kadzo threw herself flat on the deck that she realised two of the men were holding what looked like machine-guns. Split seconds later, a burst of automatic gunfire erupted across the water straight towards them.

Korir leaped across the boat, arms outstretched and in one movement, tackled Kenga who still seemed dazed to the deck. Bullets raked Safari Hatua's starboard outrigger, sending splinters into all directions. By the time Korir and the corporal had picked themselves up, whipped their pistols out of their holsters and steadied themselves to shoot at the attackers, the other boat had sped off into the horizon. Korir whistled in amazement.

"These guys are dangerous and they mean business. We need to be very careful. That was a warning and a half."

Luckily, none of them was hurt. They had to get back to the caves because Safari Hatua was badly damaged. They crossed the channel in a hurry and anchored the speedboat in shallow waters. They could not believe what had become of Safari Hatua. A friendly fisherman towed it to the kids' father's boatyard.

* * *

A week after the encounter on Safari Hatua, Kadzo and Kenga were standing outside their house when they heard a familiar engine roar. It was a speedboat. Kadzo recognised the engine noise just as a parent can recognise their baby's voice in a crowd of screaming children.

"Could it be Safari Hatua? But Safari Hatua was so shattered after the attack at Shimoni." She knew that it would cost their father thousands of shillings to repair.

Kadzo and Kenga watched in awe as the twenty-footer came into view. Its lines were so familiar. They jumped up and down with joy because it looked brand new. It had been repaired.

At the wheel piloting the boat with the help of a local fisherman was Inspector Korir. His face was wrapped with concentration as he brought the boat around.

"Easy Inspector! Watch out for those hazardous shallow draughts!" Kadzo could not help herself and shouted.

Korir navigated the boat cautiously and anchored it. The kind inspector had picked the boat earlier from Mr Karisa's yard and taken it to another mechanic. He was impressed that even the other mechanic was as experienced as the kids' father but most people preferred Karisa's yard – he had a lot of boats which needed repair. Korir was not going to delay the kids the pleasure of using their boat which was damaged by his enemies.

Chapter Fourteen

"**K**adzo, calm down," Kenga begged as they looked at the box with a human skull and two bullets.

"I can't calm down. I'm too angry. I can't believe someone can actually send us this ugly parcel just to keep us off from helping Inspector Korir with his investigations," Kenga took hold of his sister's hand.

"We need to focus and think of our next step," he urged.

"We are involved in a police investigation and it is already affecting mother adversely. We need to be careful not to blow this up because of a few threats from Mono-eye and his accomplices."

"You're right," Kadzo agreed. She took a deep breath. After all, Inspector Korir's parcel of a skinned dead cat with its tongue cut out had been more gruesome!

* * *

Later that afternoon, Inspector Korir pulled into the parking bay of the Coast Maximum Security Prison. The parking lot was more crowded than usual.

"Business must be good," he joked as the trio made the dispirited and depressing walk to the entrance. When the gates opened, they entered and stopped at the security desk.

"I'm Inspector Korir. This is Kadzo and Kenga Karisa," he did the introduction. "We have clearance to see an inmate called Musa Ibrahim."

Kadzo was led to a policewoman while Korir and Kenga were attended to by male officers. The olive-green uniformed policewoman's dour expression did not change.

"Bags," she said curtly. Kadzo put her satchel on the desk. The policewoman rifled through it, then put it on to a conveyor belt so that it could pass through an X-ray machine. The policewoman nodded towards an archway, instructing Kadzo to walk towards it. After Inspector Korir and Kenga had gone through the same process with their belongings at the hands of the male officers, a series of beeps set off when Kenga attempted to walk through the electronic archway.

Two policemen rushed towards him, their hands held up, warning him not to proceed further. Kenga backed off. One of the policemen reached for a body scanning device and waved it up and down the length of the boy's body, then patted him down. Kenga surrendered his penknife, keys and several coins before he was allowed to walk through the metal detector again. This time, there was no drama.

"Boys! Why don't you simply put that stuff in your backpack or carry nothing at all like Inspector Korir?" Kadzo rolled her eyes at him and said.

After what looked like a million years, Inspector Korir, Kenga and Kadzo were cleared by the main office and walked down a long hallway to an open courtyard and across to what looked like a small holding cell. Inside was a short man in black and white stripped prison uniform. It was Musa! His neatly folded hands rested on the table in front of him. Kadzo noticed with shock that he was still handcuffed! She wondered why the police could not remove the handcuffs after locking a suspect in a cell.

"What did you expect, silly?" She scolded herself. "This is what happens to drug peddlers like yourself!"

"You have twenty minutes," the guard told Inspector Korir as he stepped outside and closed the door, locking the three and the suspect in the same room.

"You look too young to be a brilliant lawyer," Musa commented as he looked at Korir.

"I'm not a lawyer. What made you think I'm one?" Musa leant forward, visibly upset by the presence of someone who possibly could not offer help.

"I was told a lawyer had been assigned to me. That's why I thought you were one."

Stunned Kadzo and Kenga turned to look at Korir for an explanation.

"Who could have told Musa that Korir was a lawyer?" Korir smiled wryly.

"I never actually said that I was a lawyer," he said in a hedging tone. Kadzo was so shocked. She could hardly utter her dismay. Korir had lied to get this session with Musa!

"Lied to prison officials! Was this how Kenyan cops worked? Couldn't he have simply told the truth?" Kadzo wondered.

"If you're not a lawyer then what are you doing here? What do you want from me?" Musa's eyes narrowed suspiciously. Korir unbuttoned extra buttons on his shirt. He was already sweating because of the person who sat across the table and secondly, he was not used to this coastal heat.

"Look, I'm sorry if I misled you, but ..."

"Misled me – my foot!" Musa shouted angrily. "I thought you are here to give me some legal aid. Who the hell are you?"

"I'm a police officer and my name is Inspector Korir. I just need a few answers from you. First of all, do you know these two kids?"

Musa rolled his eyes and slumped in his chair.

"Oh, great!" he groaned. "A police officer. Just what I need. Your colleagues put me in here. Why don't you go and talk to them – they have the answers you want. And yeah, I know these kids but I'm sure they've told you all there is to tell."

"I just need some more information on Big Man. I need these two kids to get back in touch with him," Korir said.

"It's a waste of time and breath. You can't catch him. For the record, I'll tell you exactly what I told the other cops, maybe you are more intelligent and will be able to do something."

* * *

"You did a great job back in there, you handled Musa like a professional journalist which is your dream, Kadzo!" Korir shouted over the wind.

Kadzo acknowledged the compliment with a lift of her chin but sat in stony angry silence at Korir's duplicity of gaining access to Musa.

"Excuse me if I don't look completely happy," she said sarcastically, "but you didn't have to lie to get to see Musa, a petty peddler. Your investigative style is – how shall I put this – unusual. Actually, I think crude is the suitable word." Kenga laughed out aloud from the back seat.

"Kadzo, what do you mean?" he gasped. "Of course, Inspector had to lie, otherwise Musa would have refused to see us."

"But at least we know from Musa despite his being incarcerated that there is a transfer going down this week. Despite being in prison, he has agreed to send word out that you two still need your old jobs with Big Man. So, if Big Man calls you guys, just go along with him and we shall nail him," Inspector Korir said. Immediately Kadzo's cell phone vibrated. It was a text message which she shared with Korir and Kenga.

"You will soon be out of this world; you and your brother. Crippled dead girl walking – your cop friend won't help you coz he will also be dead like his nosy partner. Keep your meddling long nose out of all drugs and anti-narcotics cases. This is your ticket and your family's to hell. This could be your final day – you are a dead girl limping to your death!"

Chapter Fifteen

Jamila put on her blue jeans. She then locked her room and crossed the landing to her brother's room. She looked from the landing down into the living room. It was furnished lavishly with leather sofa seats. They had everything they needed. Issa attended one of the best schools in the county although it was semi-private. They lived in a good family house in the Old Town with servants who did the cleaning, cooking and other domestic chores.

Their parents combined their income and provided everything their two children needed but it appeared as if this was not enough. There seemed to be something that had always been missing. Their doctor father came home quite late in the night and left at the crack of dawn. Their mother was so busy in her law firm. She rarely found time for the family. They could go for days without seeing one another. The children never had time to sit down with their parents to talk.

"Maybe that is why things have gone wrong with Issa," Jamila thought. She sighed wistfully as she knocked on the door to his room. They had decided to give Issa support and they were meeting with him in his room.

"Come in," Issa called out.

"Hi. What's with the long face?" Jamila asked. "I hope you are not moping."

"No." Issa said pointing to his computer which was on. "So, where are you off to today?"

"To the beach with my fiancé and later, I have to be back here early as it is henna night for me. The ladies are all excited about it. Now let's talk about you. How are you? I mean really? This is me your elder sister – remember? You can tell me anything."

"I'm fine, but things are really tough for me. I can't seem to stop craving cocaine," Issa said as he looked at his sister with desperation.

"At least, Kadzo and Kenga's parents are supportive and they are helping them."

Jamila could tell what else her brother craved for. It was obvious that her brother had started doing drugs for a completely different reason.

"After Inspector Korir, Kadzo and Kenga talked to me, I've stopped meeting up with Big Man and the other couriers but I need a replacement, someone who can give me company," Issa opened his hands as if to receive something from an imaginary source.

"Whenever I talk to Dad in search of a friend, he just goes ballistic. I mean, the old man is always on my case!" he said as he threw up the hands that had remained open for a while.

"He always has issues with me! I think I need a psychiatrist," Issa blurted.

"Thank God, I'll soon be off to the rehab. At least, I'll get some helpful therapy there and make friends!" Issa left Jamila more worried.

"Yes, you will. But I want you to know that I love you and I'll always be there for you."

A knock on the door interrupted them as Dr Abdul and his wife entered the room.

"Issa! Are you aware that one of our neighbour's son was arrested with cocaine?" Dr Abdul said as he walked towards Issa. Issa coiled.

"Mzee Juma's son was arrested and released on a ten million shillings bond. His father tells me that his son, has been ordered by the Chief Magistrate not to travel out of the county without permission," Abdul continued. Issa had closed his eyes all along. It appeared as if he was not listening to what his father was saying.

"The mention of the case has been set for next month. If convicted, Musa will face a mandatory fine of three times the value of the drugs involved," he said as he demonstrated *three* with his right hand fingers.

"This will be in addition to life imprisonment!" His last words drew Issa from his world. He shuddered.

"Issa, is this what you want to happen to you?" Dr Abdul thundered as he paced the room. Issa put his head in his hands as Jamila pulled her Dad aside.

"Dad! You are here to talk to Issa and he has already agreed to reform. He has even promised to help the police carry out the investigations. Will you please stop the drama?"

Mrs Abdul went over to Issa and hugged him.

"Son, we are so glad and we thank *Allâh* that you've decided to reform and stop using and peddling drugs. I know that we have not been here for you as parents due to our busy schedules but all that will change. I love you very much."

A discreet cough interrupted mother and son's téte â téte. Dr Abdul hovered near Issa's bed and then knelt down and took his son's hands. The old man had tears in his eyes. Jamila and Issa had never seen their father so emotional.

"Issa, my son, I'm just scared that you might get arrested." For the first time, Issa thought that he saw his father's tears.

"Juma's son was arrested at the airport with what the police say was a thousand grams of cocaine worth five million shillings. He had concealed the drugs in assorted tins and tubes of cosmetics which he said were presents for his mother and sister," Dr Abdul sighed, then continued. "I'm really glad and thank *Allâh* that you've decided to stop this dirty business and get into a rehab. I'm going to be there for you from now on. Don't ever doubt our love for you. Always talk to us."

"I'm sorry, Dad, Mum, Jamila for all the pain I've caused you. I'm serious about reforming." This was the first time the Abduls had been in the room discussing the lives of their children in a meangful way. They all hugged and soon Issa felt stronger.

"I am not going to disappoint my family any more. They love me and I must spare their tears," he told himself as he rubbed the tears in his eyes with the back of his right hand.

Chapter Sixteen

Inspector Korir was talking to Kenga, Issa and Kadzo in the parking lot of the police headquarters. Issa had finally listened to them and was leaving later that day to start his rehabilitation sessions. Kenga had recently completed this procedure and the desire to help other young people was overflowing in him. The friends had come to pay Issa a visit and give him updates on the case. The boys went round Korir's borrowed BMW.

"BMW is my favourite saloon car. You can't convince me otherwise. Whenever I'm down here, I borrow this one from a friend. I avoid moving around in a police car because they are easily noticed. This one is an E39," Korir told them.

"So this is what people call 'Be My Wife' you know, BMW!" Kenga laughed, touching the smooth metal admiringly.

"Man! It's awesome. I wonder how the new model looks like," Issa whistled.

"You bet they are awesome," the inspector said but his eyes were on Kadzo, whose silver half moon nose stud glinted in the sunlight.

"Excuse me, boys," he walked over to the girl. He was happy that she was regaining her healthy glow and looked pretty in her freshly plaited corn-rows. "Any news?" Korir looked at her and asked.

Kadzo reached her jeans back pocket and brought out a scrap of paper.

"A friend at the MV Registry helped me run a check on them. It was bought in the name of one Mustapha Jillo but it has since been sold off twice and transferred … and then the trail runs cold. This is just useless!" she lifted her hands in despair.

"Don't worry, Kadzo. I already have a lead on the name from a reliable source – security intelligence. That's why I have a date with someone at Lutfiya's Pizzeria at the seafront. I want you to go there ahead of me so that we can see if you can recognise the person I'm going to meet. I understand there have been some strange happenings at the seafront," Korir told her.

Kadzo looked at her watch.

"I hope we'll be back soon. I promised Jamila that we'll go over to her house tonight and help with her henna application. She is betrothed and soon she will be getting married," Kadzo explained.

"Let me finish up with the boys before we can go," Korir told her. He hurried to Kenga and Issa and held their shoulders.

"Well, Kenga, Issa; I don't want you boys to stop talking to your peers about the destruction and pain these drugs are causing in families. Kenga, you and Kadzo have gone through some drying out and you are already doing a lot for your community," Inspector Korir urged the boys.

"Please, talk to them about the pain you've gone through. Issa, I know you are about to check into a rehabilitation and therapy centre but you'll soon catch up with Kadzo's community work."

Issa and Kenga promised to do their best.

"We'll talk in a few days. I have to rush somewhere with Kadzo. As you've said Issa, you're off to rehab and Kenga to swimming practice. That only leaves me and Kadzo to battle with the drug barons!"

Chapter Seventeen

K orir was holding Kadzo's shoulder. He gave her a pat.

"I hope you'll be careful, Inspector," Kadzo told him.

He opened his jacket giving her a glimpse of his cell phone.

"Of course, call me in case of any problem."

"Don't get lost," she warned anyway. "I'll be waiting for you. Please, hurry and don't forget the signpost, just before the Florida Nightclub. It will show you the way to the venue."

Later in the evening, Kadzo decided to take a walk. It was almost six. The gentle breeze was beckoning her to keep on walking. She walked along the edge of the cliffs and stared into the horizon. In the course of doing that, she glimpsed a ship leaving the port. She did not give it any attention; after all, many ships docked and left. She walked further on wishing the two hours they had agreed on with Korir would fly quickly.

She went over to the sea wall packed with hawkers and bought some roast cassava. She had hardly taken two bites when the frisson of unease crept up her spinal cord; she felt as if someone was watching her. She looked around but there was no one. Strangely, the unseen eyes did not seem to close.

She decided to go down the cliffs and look for those cement benches to sit on. She had done that lots of times but today, it was extremely difficult because one of her legs was now artificial. She glanced twice from the corner of her eye. She was now sure that two men were following her. It was almost dark. It had also started drizzling and soon the showers developed into a steady downpour.

She peered over the edge of the cliff to see if the men had gone. She did not see them but her instincts refused to believe that they had gone. Her exposed skin now slick with rain, her damp clothes clinging to her skin, Kadzo took a few steps through the wet grass. She got down on her knees when she heard the men's voices. Sitting back on her haunches, she took a deep breath. Something else was distracting her; it kept hovering at the back of her mind, but she could not put her finger on it.

"I have to remember what it is. Concentrate damn it!" She began again, slower this time, her senses attuned not only to her surroundings but also to the elusive shadows she kept glimpsing flitting through the foliage. Then she remembered! She felt the back pocket of her skinny jeans; her cell phone was missing.

"Oh my God! I knew something was amiss! No wonder it's been nagging at the back of my mind! How could I?! I am the one who was telling Korir to be careful," she wished she was back in the warmth of her mother's kitchen!

She hurriedly got to her feet when she heard twigs creaking behind her. Where the hell was Korir? She was sure that two hours were already over. Chilled to the bone from both rain and fear, she wrapped her hands around herself and tried to back off. The slippery grass caught her off-guard; she did a fancy dance to stay upright as she tried to steady herself. She heard the creaking of twigs again. "Oh please, God let it be Korir and not these thugs I keep conjuring up!" she prayed silently.

Back on her knees, she felt the rain-soaked path beneath her with both hands and grazed them as she held on to the jagged edges of the cliff. She settled on to a ledge she felt with her feet – her triumph died an immediate death when she heard a sucking sound behind her. Her heart skipped a beat. A shoe pulling free of the mud! Charged with adrenaline, she tried getting to her feet gingerly so as not to slip off the ledge but it was not easy with her artificial leg. Whoever was behind her was faster. He hit her hard in the middle of her back before she could straighten herself properly on the ledge. A terrified Kadzo screamed as she slipped off the edge into the empty space!

* * *

Meanwhile Korir was racing back along Mama Ngina Drive. He could not believe that he had seen Big Man entering the Imperial Kings' Lodge further up along the drive – a courtesy call on the visiting king who was officially in the country to open the embassy.

"The government officials in the country know that he was a known drug baron for heaven's sake and yet they give him access into high profile public offices!" Korir hit the steering wheel as he stepped on the accelerator harder than before. "Why am I sure that I am being followed? Who is following me?" he asked no one.

"Are they Big Man's henchmen after they had dropped him off at the Imperial King's Lodge? Are they the stevedores who had warned Kadzo and I off?"

So many questions went through Korir's mind. Adrenaline pumped through his arteries, urging him to drive faster. Even though the rain was blinding him and the windscreen wipers were working at a furious rate, he dared press the fuel pad.

It was like a fog – he guessed it was because of the sea. The fog's tentacles embraced everything in its path, swallowing objects whole. Cafés ... the Florida Casino ... houses .... trees ... he could not see a thing! Not even the signpost for Lutfiya's Pizzeria, the landmark they had agreed he would pick Kadzo up! To make matters worse, he was not very familiar with this part of town. Though he had switched the car lights to full bright, the beam barely cut a path through the sheets of rain which was now coming down in torrents! Considering the conditions, he was driving recklessly and he knew it but he could not think about his own safety. Not when he had left Kadzo a sitting duck – whoever was following him must have tracked them down earlier, seen them together and obviously knew where he had left Kadzo. This was a well-set trap! They had known he would not resist planning this with Kadzo.

A thin beam of light reflected in his rear-view mirror. It was another car creeping up on him as he swerved around a hairpin turn. "I am not the only one driving like a mad man," he thought wryly. "... probably, the only one who doesn't know the road though!" His stomach churned. A fist closed around his heart when he thought of Kadzo: alone and vulnerable, undoubtedly not even considering the danger she might be in. At the moment, he could only concentrate on getting to her side as fast as possible. Korir swore when he noticed that the distance between his BMW and the dark car behind him had narrowed.

"Is that driver crazy?" Korir tapped his brake pedal lightly a few times in warning but the driver was either not aware of the flashing red lights or he was ignoring them. Up an incline and around a curve, the other vehicle stayed with him. He decided to press hard on the accelerator. His mind was in a whirlwind! What was the other driver trying to do? Was he trying to kill him? All he could see to his right was the deep blue sea, the jagged cliffs and the Likoni Ferry landing in the far distance! Gaining speed down the sharp incline did as much damage to his stomach as any case of food poisoning could do but at least he had put some distance between him and the other car. Fear gripped him again, not for himself but for Kadzo.

The vehicle following him zoomed forward again, more quickly this time, as if the other driver was only keen on overtaking him. Realising the potential danger, Korir scanned the side of the road for a widening. A pull over. Anything. Nothing! All that met his eyes was an impression of a drop-off. He looked to his left, all he could see were children walking home hurriedly from the playground. He was in danger and these children were also in great danger. Hawkers who had been selling roast cassava and maize and were now loading their wares onto wooden handcarts were also in great danger. Korir also risked a head-on collision with the truck coming the other way! Not much of a choice. Blinded for a moment by the full lights of the oncoming truck, he swerved to his far right. His wheels were on the edge of the road, too close for comfort as the truck roared on.

He pulled the BMW back a bit, not quite to the centre line, giving the driver following him a chance to pass but while the gap narrowed dangerously, the other vehicle stayed directly behind him. His gut clenching ominously, Korir knew that Kadzo was not the only one in trouble ... He now sensed that the other driver did not want to pass or overtake him. The first jolt threw him forward. Though he was unprepared for a game of bumping cars, his seat belt prevented his chest from being crushed against the wheel. Suddenly, the light house loomed out of the darkness and immediately, he noticed a sharp curve on the road. He steered the car around it as he was rammed again and again from behind, harder this time. Intuition or an inner voice told him to open his windows and unbuckle his seat belt. He managed to let go the steering wheel for a while to do the necessary with his seat belt and the automatic switch for the windows; who knows? The way things were, he would end up in the deep blue sea! He suddenly remembered a passage in Bilal's dossier.

"...independent minded investigators are killed and their partners lose motivation to continue – some are shot outside their gates and nothing is stolen from them. Family members who squeal on their kin's dirty business and witnesses who report to dirty cops are killed instantly once they are labelled as informers..."

He prayed that Kadzo would not die because she had tried to help him! Korir braced himself for the inevitable as he glanced over the edge. His neck snapped painfully and his head flew back. He threw a glance at the rear-view mirror. His suspicions were justified when he caught the familiar silhouette of one of Big Man's henchmen in the driver's seat of the black car. A final hit sent the BMW careering out of his control over the edge and onto the jagged rocks of the cliffs and into the wide, deep sea below.

Chapter Eighteen

Korir was in extreme pain. He looked around realising that he had been thrown out of the car before it hit the water. Was it luck or God's hand that he had had the instinct to open the window and unfasten his seat belt? He was lucky that he had landed on a grassy incline and not the jagged corals. An incessant beeping kept intruding on his mind. After a minute, he realised that it was his cell phone! Where was it? It was not in his pockets. It must be on the grass somewhere!

The luminous blue glow of his phone's screen lit up in a clump of bushes. He rushed, groped around and managed to retrieve it. He saw Kenga's name flashing on the screen.

"Kenga! Thank God, it's you!"

"Why? What's up?!" Kenga exclaimed.

"Never mind!" Korir said. "Please, call the police and let them know that there's been an accident on Mama Ngina Drive. Someone tried to kill me and pushed my car into the ocean. I was lucky to be thrown out. I have a feeling Kadzo is in deep trouble. I left her at Lutfiya's. Please, hurry."

"Ok. No wonder I've been trying to reach her on her mobile in vain," Kenga said.

Korir hurriedly scrolled his phone book and dialed Kadzo's number. She was unreachable.

Korir cursed silently as he listened to the computerised voice of the Safaricom mobile service provider before it diverted and switched to voice-mail. He remembered that Kadzo's phone had been on. He realised that she must have lost it or she was in serious trouble!

"Has the battery charge run down?" he prayed that it was the latter.

He dialed the police hotlines and, ironically, all were busy. He looked around and noticed that he was near the beach line. Thank God it was low-tide! He looked up the incline and knew that Lutfiya's was up on the road and that he would have to walk along the beach line and look for footholds on the cliffs then go up. This way, he would be able to look for Kadzo. With his heart pounding with misgiving, he walked up some jutting rocks trying to avoid the slick and steep incline. By some miracle, he avoided the cliffs and stayed on his feet near the sea wall.

"Where could Kadzo be? Anything could have happened to her," he tried to gauge the distance from the rocky incline to Lutfiya's Pizzeria by the roadside.

Fear threatened to choke him when he heard sharp slap-slap of feet stomping away. His chest squeezed tight until he heard a faint cry from the other side. There was hope. This assured him that at least Kadzo was alive. He had to get to her fast. Envisioning her in free-fall and plunging into the Indian Ocean made his stomach twist into knots.

"Kadzo! Where are you?" he called out. Though he knew she had to be close by, he barely heard her over the heaving of his own laboured breath and the sweeping winds.

"I can't ... hang on ... much longer ...," he heard her gasping voice. Bile welled in his throat. He pushed it down together with what he thought was his heart. He soon found himself up by the road and looked down into the inky blackness. He walked around trying to locate the direction of her voice.

"I'm ... I'm down here on this ledge ... "

"Kadzo! Hang on! I'm coming!" he shouted down to her. The rain was letting up and his eyes were adjusting. He could not believe that just a few minutes ago, he had sped past this spot with the black car on his tail yet Kadzo had been in trouble!

He got a vague impression of the clearing even as he heard a series of twig-like creaking sounds, followed by a swallowed scream coming directly from his left. Wasting no time, he threw himself down face first, his stomach skimming the ground as his head and shoulders thrust over the edge forgetting that he had hurt his head when he was thrown out of the car. Her flimsy green top caught his eye – she was directly below him!

He could hear her panting ... her body slipping ... her fingers scrabbling for a better hold. He pushed forward as far as he dared – his shoulders and upper torso hanging over the edge. Two men heard Korir call out. Thanks to the kind nature of the people of this city, one of the coconut sellers brought his climbing rope and gave it to him. The rocky trail along the edge of the ridges was very precarious. The cliffs were straight up and Korir could see that there was only about 10 inches for Kadzo to put her feet. His heart was in his mouth. Just one mis-step and she would drop off the cliff and die. The noise from the wind and the soaring waves below was loud. Korir had to use his free hand to communicate to Kadzo. The hand holds were slippery. Kadzo grabbed at a rock that looked less slippery but it broke loose. She lost her grip and her feet slipped at the same time. She just managed to find another foothold on time.

"I'll get you!" he yelled, his voice competing with the wind. The clump of shrubbery Kadzo was hanging onto also broke free of the wet earth that had formed from the rocks. She started to slide. His arm shot towards her but he could not reach way down to clamp around her wrist.

"Kadzo! Please! Don't give up! You've got to help me!"

"I'm … trying …," he tried to think because he could not let go of her. Suddenly, her voice sharpened.

"Oh no! the coral has crumbled away! It was rotten! Korir, I'm gonna die!" she gasped.

"No you won't die! I won't let you! Feel around for another foothold!" he commanded.

"I can't!"

Though her body was flush against the outcrop of jutting rocks, the pitch of the incline on the other hand was like a slope.

Korir knew she was fighting gravity, valiantly seeking a new hold of some kind.

"Her hands must be bleeding by now ... these sharp corals ...," he thought. Gritting his teeth, he took a mental step beyond the pain. Finally, her jerky movements subsided. For a moment, they both remained immobile, pausing to draw some breath, panting in unison.

"I found a foothold with my one foot!" she gasped out. "Now what?"

"Find something stronger above your head to grab onto with your other hand," he ordered. "...and please! please! for heaven's sake, don't dare look down into the sea below!"

He knew instinctively that the last thing she wanted to do was to move. He also knew she was a no quitter. He felt her carefully adjust herself. Sliding. He felt her other hand clawing, fingers digging in.

"Korir! I told you ... the ledge crumbled away. It's more of slippery mud than rock! I only have a toe hold on a small rock," he could hear the tears in her voice.

"Listen to me. Don't cry! That small rock will hold you," he assured her. "It has to."

There were more desperate clawing noises. Korir was not a particularly religious man but he prayed like he had never before. He vowed to God that he would attend Mass every Sunday ... and every evening prayer ... participate in Novenas ... even make a Pilgrimage to the Holy Land using his next pay cheque ... anything... if only she would be alright. He had got her into this mess … damn it! He could not imagine himself facing her family if anything bad happened.

Finally, she croaked, "Got it!"

"What!?" he croaked back, startled out of his reverie.

"Another foothold! What else do you think?".

"Alright!" he told her. "I'm edging towards you and will tie your left arm to this rope." Kadzo looked up and saw the fear on Korir's face. He tried to conceal it with his 'Superman' courage in vain. Luckily, her feet struck a stronger foothold. She was no longer on slippery rocks. She also got a handhold on another ledge and hang on.

Korir found a handhold on another ledge too and tied the rope to its jutting ledge. He then dropped the rope to Kadzo. She looked at him and shook her head. She then looked at her hands and he understood. She was not in a position to let go the ledge and hold the rope.

Korir stretched as far as he could without letting go of his left handhold on the ledge. He then motioned Kadzo to try and pull herself upward but Kadzo was still scared to let go.

Korir dangled his body dangerously over the ledge as far as he could go. With one hand, he was able to tie the end of the rope to Kadzo's left arm. He motioned that he'd tied the rope to a solid rock on the ledge and that it would not slip off.

Kadzo trusted him. She let go and grabbed the rope with her right hand. As she let go, she felt her foot slip. Whatever had been holding her foot in place had crumbled away. She let out a gasp and screamed as she started to fall off the edge of the cliff. Luckily, the rope tied to her hand held her in place, dangling in mid-air.

"Kadzo! Don't fear! The rope is holding you. Push up and I'll back off. Together, one, two, go!" Korir's voice pierced the air. He managed to retreat several inches, enough to give himself more leverage.

Hope gave him strength. Kadzo slowly started inching herself upwards. Inch by inch. Painfully. It looked as if it took hours getting back to the topmost ledge. Her hands were burning because of the strain of the rope. Her arms felt like they had been torn off their sockets. They repeated the process until Korir could grab her wrists and maintain his balance. Though he was bracing himself, he was not ready for the force of her weight jerking him. He hung onto her for all he was worth.

Pain meant nothing as he dragged her up and onto him. Throwing her arms around his neck, she clung to him as if she would never let go. Her face was streaked with tears. He had never had such reason to be thankful in his entire life. That is when they heard the sirens!

"The blasted cops are finally on the way!" Korir said. "I talked to your brother a while ago and asked him to call the cops. But you know what, Kadzo? You need to get into the good books of Big Man again so that we can get a breakthrough in this case."

Korir started explaining to her what had transpired from the time he had left her at Lutfiya's. She also explained to him how she had ended up on the ledge and not in the water below.

"Thank God you are okay!" he said.

"I thank God you are too."

That is when they became aware that they were surrounded by people who had been silently cheering Korir on as he rescued Kadzo. A television crew arrived soon with the cameras rolling.

"Don't look so surprised Korir," Kadzo chided. "Cops are always the last to arrive at crime scenes!" she wrapped her arms around herself shivering with the cold as she was soaked to the skin.

Soon Kenga arrived. Half an hour later the cops emerged, last to arrive as usual. They were swarming all over the place and a police yellow crime scene tape was established.

"Have they just arrived or they were hiding in the bushes waiting for the difficult task to be completed?" This thought could not leave Korir alone. He wondered why they were codorning off the cliff.

"Now that I'm in the journalism club, this will be my first story for our school paper!" Kadzo proclaimed.

"Why don't we all go and have warm baths, and a good night's sleep? Now my henna application date with Jamila is no more," Kadzo said. Nobody argued with her as they all trooped to the taxi bay outside Lutfiya's Pizzeria. Kenga and Kadzo agreed with Korir and the police that they would go to the station in the morning to record statements on the incidents.

Chapter Nineteen

There was a faint hint of the forest smell drifting over the beach after the storm. An almost eerie silence from the direction of the Kaya Forest seemed to give voice to the calamity that had befallen the city. It appeared as if the spirits of the ancestors resting in this forest seemed displeased by the drugs that were threatening their lineage.

This particular day, Kadzo had helped organise a *baraza* with the support of the area chief. The Kaya elders were in full support of this move. Most people seemed to have realised that they were perishing because of ignorance. They wished that their day's actions would open the eyes of the people of Diani. Many youth were in the throes of addiction. Imams and pastors from several villages had converged here for a one day *baraza*, to talk to their people about one thing. The Kaya elders wanted one thing in particular: to bring the youth back to the social sanity that once existed before the current pollution.

Speaker after speaker took on to the podium and it emerged that police operations had failed to stop the entry of drugs into the county. Victims decried the delay in dispensing drug-related cases in courts.

Kadzo was given a chance to speak to the audience about her experience in the circles of drug trafficking and abuse. After giving her short speech, she introduced two young men whom she had counselled and assisted out of the snare. Their tales were shocking.

"I was born into a wealthy family. Being the only heir, my late father bequeathed me property worth millions of shillings," he said as he fidgeted.

"I started taking drugs five years ago and I would spend almost twenty thousand shillings a day," he was interrupted by the noises of surprise from the crowd, "... seeking this false satisfaction. I would spend most of my time with a syringe of heroin stuck in my arm or just sniffing cocaine day and night." He pulled up the sleeves of his shirt and showed the audience the needle marks on his once light skin. "I sold the property I had inherited from my father at throw away prices," he said.

"As I speak, I have nothing to show for it. I even sold the three tuk tuks which I had bought. My family members have disowned me and thrown me out into the streets."

"Ooh! What a shame!" the audience sighed.

"Despite my addiction and destructive habits, I did get married," he said this with a lot of pride, his voice gaining more and more confidence. "I got a son and a daughter but my wife separated from me and took our children because she could not stand my habits. When nothing of all I once had was left, I started stealing from family members. I regret getting into drugs but I'm now undergoing rehabilitation. I encourage young people not to try drugs," the second man's story was not any better.

"My friend just told me to have a puff of heroin and I obliged," he started off. "It was the beginning of a long road to misery and hopelessness because it led me to addiction." As he demonstrated with his hands, the tremor in his muscles was visible. One could tell that he was still suffering from the withdrawal symptoms.

"I was a fisherman then and the habit I took on changed me. To function on any given chore in my daily life, I had to be intoxicated. I needed a lot of money to sustain my habit." He looked down. Kadzo touched him and whispered to him to continue.

"That is when I started selling household items," he said and broke down in tears.

"The whole family turned against me. When word spread on the island that I had joined the network of drug users, the police put me on the list of wanted persons. I was rejected by the entire community and society at large." As he said this, he recoiled and walked two steps backwards, then continued.

"I resorted to other measures to ensure I would not miss my daily dose of heroin. This is when I sold my dhow – my main source of income. When my best friend died due to an overdose, I resolved to quit the habit and talked to my family. They finally decided to salvage whatever was left of my life and offered to enroll me into a rehabilitation centre. I accepted their offer immediately. Now I have reformed. I want to help other people in the snare to break off. I have witnessed so many people die owing to drug abuse related causes. Many lives have also been completely destroyed by the vice but for those who still have an opportunity to live right, they can make the most of it." The audience was moved by the testimony of the once drug abusers.

Later, Kadzo distributed pamphlets and fliers to enlighten the audience about the withdrawal symptoms of drug abuse.They gave insights to both the addicts and the care givers. The audience was shocked to know that the way to recovery was not all rosy as those hooked to the habit are prone to suffer once a drug is withdrawn. Parents testified to have seen their children exhibit abnormal physical and psychological symptoms after abrupt discontinuation of a drug. They were able to understand why doctors administered anti-depressants to patients during rehabilitation.

"Symptoms are painful and can kill within days if necessary measures are not taken," Dr Abdul told the audience and encouraged them to have addicts undergo professional rehabilitation.

"Excessive sweating, tremors, vomiting, anxiety, insomnia, diarrhoea and muscle pain can cause death," he told them. Other young people who had successively undergone rehabilitation jumped in to share their experiences.

"There are obvious signs and symptoms to watch for in teenagers hooked to drugs," Kadzo said. Some give up past activities like sports and dedication to homework," Kadzo allowed the audience time to reflect.

"Most people, especially teenagers start hanging out with new friends and register declining grades," she said, dropping her voice. "If they are involved in peddling, they all of a sudden start having lots of excess money."

"Forgetfulness, aggressiveness and irritability, feeling run down, hopelessness, depression and suicidal threats, selfishness, personal neglect to hygiene, use of air fresheners, incense in their rooms if they were not using such are other signs that one could be a drug user," she explained.

"I have personally done all those things but unfortunately, my parents did not suspect a thing," Hassan alarmed the audience with his confession. His mother pierced the silence that followed with a shrill scream and disrupted the *baraza*. The participant turned their attention to her as she fell down and fainted.

"Many addicts start using perfumes, deodorants and chewing gum – to conceal or disguise the smell of drugs; they get drunk on a regular basis more than ever before, and keep small snuff boxes, pipes and rolling paper; lying about how much alcohol or other drugs they take and engaging in risky sexual behaviours with a belief that to have fun, one must drink or use other drugs to be on a constant high…," Hassan went on as he peered through the audience. Two girls walked to the front and stood next to him.

"Do not worry," he said, pointing his finger to the girls who nodded in the affirmation. "These are my friends and as good friends, we are now fighting our common enemy together."

A cold breeze from the Kaya Forest swept over the audience as if in agreement that drug use and addiction should be wiped out of the coastal city and that all drug barons should be swallowed by the sea.

After a few minutes of pondering over what Kadzo and others had just said, and relating it to what they saw in their sons and daughters, the parents were stirred. They asked many questions to gain more clarity and understanding. In the end, the gathering was divided into an impromptu workshop by Dr Abdul and Dr Otieno who had volunteered to be assisting with counselling at the rehabilitation centre.

Chapter Twenty

Walking home from the *baraza*, Mrs Karisa held Kadzo's hand and strolled beside her husband and son.

"My children, I am so proud of you. What you are doing for other teenagers and their families is commendable and very brave. I'm sorry that you lacked some basic necessities but I want to assure you that we love you very much and now that I feel better, I will do my best to provide all that you need."

"Oh, Mother! We are the ones who should be sorry for what we put you and Father through. I could have died in that shark attack but God helped me. We thank *Allâh* that we are all well," Kadzo said.

Mr Karisa, who had been eavesdropping moved closer and hugged his family.

"I am the one who should be thankful to *Allâh* because you risked your very lives to provide for us when we lacked. All the money I was getting was going towards your mother's medications. Now, I'm glad that the government has waived Kadzo's hospital bill. My children, always know that we are here for you and you can talk to us about anything. Don't ever go back to your old habits, especially now that you have gone through rehabilitation and you are now clean!"

"We won't Father!" Kadzo and Kenga said in unison. The whole family burst out laughing.

"But first we have to help Inspector Korir bust Big Man's cartel!" Kadzo quipped.

Dr Abdul and his family caught up with the Karisas, who had invited the Abduls for the *baraza* and Dr Abdul had agreed partly because he could see the good work the teenagers were doing. He also wanted Issa to join them as soon as he came back from the rehab. The Karisas' home was nearby and soon Mrs Karisa was ushering Dr Abdul and Mrs Abdul into their sparsely furnished living room. She went into the kitchen with Kadzo to prepare tea. Mrs Abdul volunteered to help.

The men's voices carried over into the kitchen as they talked.

"What about the Lamborghini and other luxury cars impounded during last year's hashish saga, Dr Abdul was heard saying. "They are still languishing at the Special Criminals Department headquarters even after the owner, a known drug baron was gunned down abroad...."

Mr Karisa looked thoughtful as he answered Dr Abdul.

"I'm just sorry that it had to take drug addiction and peddling by our children and a shark attack on Kadzo for me to realize what a serious toll drug trafficking has had on families." Kadzo's father was openly worried by the recent happenings.

"*Allâh,* help us!" Mrs Abdul exclaimed. "But you know what? I am yet to understand this shark thing. Poor Kadzo! How on earth did the shark appear at the South Coast and what on earth happened to the dolphins?"

"I'm more conversant with fishing matters and I can tell you that sharks, especially if they are hungry, usually follow freighters, cruise ships and trawlers into the port," his knowledge of the sea was commendable. Abdul looked at him with admiration.

"Two weeks ago, local fishermen caught one of those harmless sharks, the plankton eaters off the waters of Bamburi. It is not a strange occurrence. They also follow the North Easterly Monsoon winds. They really like the nutrient rich waters on the coast because it contains fish," Mrs Karisa explained as she carried the tea into the living room.

"First, it was the proliferation of small arms, practically everywhere in our estates and now these drug kingpins are everywhere!" Mrs Abdul clicked her tongue in disgust.

Kadzo and Issa helped serve the tea as the conversation moved onto the police investigation the kids were helping out with and what it involved.

Chapter Twenty one

Kadzo had done as Inspector Korir had suggested and she was here once again to courier the cargo that had been prepared. All it had taken was for Musa to send word to the grapevine that Kadzo and Kenga were again looking for jobs as couriers and Big Man, unable to resist, had contacted them. The shipping trawler had this time come in from the high seas with more than thirty frozen shark carcasses. This day, Kenga was bait boy. Big Man always preferred Kadzo to be navigator more than bait girl because she was more adept at maneuvering round the corals in comparison to Kenga, when it came to Safari Hatua. Kadzo had developed a phobia for sharks after losing her leg and was grateful she was far away from the carcasses!

Kenga admitted to himself that what he was doing was better than helping his father fillet fish for the market the whole day. He plunged the fillet knife into the soft underbelly of one dead shark and expertly, the way *baba* had taught them, cut upwards towards the mouth and then removed the guts which he threw into a bucket nearby. He worked quickly and efficiently through the thirty carcasses. The stevedores then took over, filling the now empty bellies of the sharks with slabs of cocaine. All the thirty carcasses were soon stuffed with the goods of trade and sewn up again and refrigerated in the coolers in the hold of the ship, awaiting their shipment abroad.

Kadzo and Kenga watched as the stevedores worked, stuffing packaged cocaine into brand new computer speakers, soles of new shoes, linings of new leather jackets and traditional African drums with the hollow centres covered with dry hide. Some sachets of cocaine were even weaved into baskets! Kadzo wondered what Inspector Korir would make of these new methods of drug mules. Some parcels of cocaine were put into cartons containing vegetables of red and green chilli pepper and labelled as fresh produce destined for the United Kingdom.

As Kadzo pretended to mop the deck of the mother-ship, she observed all this. She watched from the corner of her eye as the approaching boat controlled by one of Mono-eye's henchmen draw nearer. She identified it as a high-powered speedboat, the kind she sometimes saw moored near the rich tourist resorts at Kikambala and Watamu; the kind that she dreamt of owning one day. There was a white man hunched beside the wheel behind the windshield. The boat drew alongside the larger ship and Kenga tossed a mooring rope to the white man as instructed by Mono-eye. As the white man took the rope, Kenga secured it to one of the deck cleats. Kadzo watched as the white man clambered up the whitewashed ladder on the side of the ship.

"What are you two morons staring at?" Mono-eye shouted. "Load the cargo into your speedboat pronto! Idiots!"

Kadzo and Kenga hurriedly went below deck and came back with the packets of carefully packed cocaine labelled Kenyan Coffee and loaded them onto Safari Hatua which was on the starboard side of the ship.

"Make sure you drop off the stuff at the right place. Okay?"

"Yes boss!" Kadzo and Kenga replied simultaneously as they pocketed the bundles of crisp one thousand shilling notes that Mono-eye gave them. Mono-eye did not believe in paper work. He expected as always that Kadzo and Kenga would memorise the instructions and directions of the drop-off point as if they were military orders.

"One mistake kids and you are both dead," he extended the fore finger of his right hand like a cocked pistol and pointed at them. Then Mono-eye said something to the white man in the other speedboat which was also full of the cargo. The craft's mighty engines coughed into life. Kadzo and Kenga watched as the mother ship moved away in a lazy arc. They saw its stern bite into the churning water, the turbo kicked in and it fired its way towards the even further high seas. Kadzo steered their boat towards the distant mainland of Kinango. They had the information that Korir needed.

Kadzo sighed listlessly as she was brought back to earth by Kenga's antics at the wheel of their speedboat. It was not a cheap one. It would have taken their father thirty years of fishing income to buy. Kenga had now mastered the steering and eased forward the throttles as he laughed aloud with childish pleasure at the throb of the engine. Kadzo kept thinking about their drug peddling in the past year and that the only other source of income that had kept them going was what their father, the best dhow repairer and boat mechanic on the entire Kenyan seaboard brought home. His drag-netting for marlin and tuna, two hundred miles into the high seas almost every day did not bring in much income. *Mama's* hospital bills consumed much of this. She took over the wheel of the boat they had christened Safari Hatua. The name was ironic – the truth was, it had cost Big Man a few million shillings to buy it for them. She gently nosed Safari Hatua round the headland and steered the boat for mooring up to the private jetty of Mr Piero Domenico. This was where they were to drop the drugs and get yet another huge payment.

"To hell with Mono-eye!" Kenga shouted. "How dare he call us morons? How dare he talk to us like that? Does he think he's the Sultan of Mombasa or what? I'm glad that this is the last time we are dealing with him. I hope the cops get him tomorrow night!"

Chapter Twenty two

A s Kadzo peered over to where the four military trucks were parked, she wondered where Kenga and Inspector Korir were. They were supposed to have met her here half an hour ago. She moved closer to the perimeter fence and saw that there were two army officers standing guard over the convoy. Both of them clutched the AK-47s that were slung over their shoulders. Big Man came out of the camp with a senior officer, guessing from the colour and design of his uniform. It was different from the two guarding the military trucks.

Mono-eye shouted instructions to the two officers. They ran to the back of the first truck in the convoy and unlocked the rear doors. Mono-eye and his partner looked inside and nodded with satisfaction. The officers slammed the doors shut and all of them left as if going into the barracks.

Kadzo waited until they had completely gone out of sight and then limped over to the fence which had now been left unmanned. It had been about three months since she got her artificial left leg and so she was able to nimbly climb over from the far side and run over to the truck whose doors the officers had opened for Mono-eye. She went to the rear of the truck and opened one of the doors and clambered inside to have a look. The interior was dark but stacked high with white carton boxes labelled: ORIGINAL KENYAN COFFEE – DESTINATION UK. These were the same boxes they had couriered over from the ship and dropped at Mr Piero Domenico's home. They had been right in their eavesdropping on Big Man's conversation. They had heard that the same consignment would be departing from these barracks via a convoy. She took her penknife from her jeans pocket and neatly cut open the top of one of the cartons. She then reached inside and pulled out one of the nylon packets. She pierced it open and sniffed at the white powder. Pure crack! It meant that all the four trucks in the convoy were filled with cocaine with just a packet or two of coffee to fool any official who would come snooping by; though it was highly unlikely in an army barracks.

The truck was stuffy but had two tiny air ventilation slots in the roof. She froze when she heard voices – Mono-eye and his partners were back! There was no way she could clamber out of the truck and limp to the fence without being seen! She had to stay put – all she had time for was to slide the truck doors shut and fasten them using the inside bolt handle and pray that they did not realise that anything was amiss. After doing exactly that, she flattened herself against the doors and held them for dear life, praying that they did not notice the outside bolt was not closed. The footsteps came closer and Kadzo froze as a shadow passed in front of the tiny crack between the two doors. If they attempted to open the doors, she would be dead!

Thankfully, the soldiers did not double-check the doors as was their habit and they remained shut and locked from inside. After some moment had elapsed, she felt a lurch as Mono-eye and the senior officer climbed into the front cabin of the truck — the same truck Kadzo had holed in. The only light came in from the tiny ventilations above her head, a narrow sliver of brightness in pitch darkness. The metal panels of the truck shook, followed by the grating rumble of a motor and the engine kicked into life. The floor beneath her feet began to vibrate and Kadzo's brief moment of relief that she had not been caught was now overtaken by dread that she was trapped in the moving truck. All she could do was pray that Kenga had gotten there on time to see the convoy leaving and, hopefully, seen her climb into the truck.

Kadzo was shocked at the duplicity and extent of crime but then, she was not surprised because their father always told them that there are bound to be a few bad apples on every good tree. He would not use apples as an example all the time but he would say that the rotting of a fish begins from the head. Indeed, many government institutions had started to rot and this would soon spread to the citizens.

After what looked like ages, Kadzo fell asleep. A lurch of the truck over several speed bumps jolted her awake. The luminous dial on her waterproof diver's watch told her that they had been travelling for an hour and a half, the smooth ride indicated that they were most probably headed inland on the country's few main arterial roads. Most probably, towards the Mombasa-Nairobi Highway. The heat in the metal-lined military truck was unbearable and the stump that was her knee strapped to the artificial leg started to ache. Her T-shirt was soaked in sweat and she thought she would soon suffocate to death as the vent was not providing enough air.

After a while, the truck slowed down. The engine rattled and died. Kadzo remained very still. She thought they would come and open the truck doors but instead, she heard the truck's front doors slam, followed by Mono-eye's voice and the other officers retreating into the distance. She waited for a few minutes, in case one of the junior officers stationed by the convoys with his AK-47 gun was outside. Then fumbling in the dark, she found the inside bolt handle and opened the lock. Bright sunshine flooded the truck's interior almost blinding her but she managed to tumble onto the ground. She scrambled under the vehicle and crawled to the side of the truck, expecting at any time, to hear gunfire and shouts of alarm. Thankfully, the only sound she could hear was that of the wind passing through the palm tree fronds.

The trucks were parked outside what appeared to be a warehouse, a hundred or so metres from the highway that sliced through the bushy savannah landscape. On the gate, a sign was painted in black capital letters: TRANSCARGO BONDED WAREHOUSE. The army officers were nowhere in sight. She had no idea of where she was. The only landmark was the highway. She ran behind the row of parked trucks, keeping low and out of sight, and on towards a rickety barbed wire fence that was broken in some sections and slipped into the highway.

She glimpsed a few isolated huts whose roofs were thatched with palm tree fronds.

She guessed that she had been right and they were somewhere in the coastal villages of Mazeras or Mariakani. She limped alongside the road lined with telegraph poles supporting thick loops of vandalised cable wires. She had to find out where she was and call Kenga and inspector Korir.

There was no telephone booth in sight and no one to ask where she was. She did not have a mobile phone either. She trudged and limped along the highway for a few minutes and then sat down despondently on a lonely stretch. Suddenly, Inspector Korir's borrowed BMW screeched to a halt right beside her, in the front passenger seat sat a beaming Kenga.

"Pull over ahead at the fence under that huge Safaricom billboard, just before you get to the reservoir road. I'll tell you all about my adventure. Where were you two?" relieved, Kadzo asked.

"You should thank us. We got to the barracks in time to see the convoy pulling away. We had a feeling you were hiding inside one of the trucks, or worse that Big Man had caught you!" Kenga exclaimed.

Listening to Kadzo's update, Korir was not surprised in the least bit by the fact that there were a few rotten apples in the military, just like there was in the police force. Bilal's dossier - about military escorts being used by drug barons was turning out to be true. He followed Kadzo's directions and cruised off the exit that led to the interchange and pulled onto the shoulder of the road beneath the green, red and white billboard.

Chapter Twenty three

The following night, a long black trailer nosed its way into the TransCargo Bonded Warehouse. The truck came to a stop outside Number 10. The driver and several other young men rushed out and opened the steel doors. They got inside and started lifting the pallets containing 'Kenyan Coffee on Transit'.

Suddenly, sirens blasted through the night and there was a crashing noise outside the steel doors. The metallic sound of alarm bells shrieked through the quiet of the building. A guard on the ground floor who was initially immobile dashed for the telephone on the wall. Another guard came from the interior of the warehouse and double-locked the steel doors from inside.

A shocked and startled Big Man knew what that meant. Nosy! Nosy unentrepreneural souls! He clicked his tongue and ran towards a stairway that led to the fire escape but first, he had to do some cleaning. He poured a jerry can of petrol which was always hidden in a corner onto the floor of the warehouse and struck a matchstick. He then rushed and climbed the staircase to the roof of the warehouse. A helicopter was parked on a helipad at the centre of the roof. Big Man ran towards it with Inspector Korir in hot pursuit but he was way ahead of the Inspector. He jumped into the chopper and raced the engine. On the premises of the warehouse two police cars were racing towards the direction of the flying helicopter. A burst of bullets crashed around the chopper but it rose into the air and continued rising into the sky until it disappeared with Big Man onboard. It seemed that the bullets had not gotten the fuselage; otherwise the copter would have burst into flames.

The warehouse was locked and engulfed in flames with workers trapped inside. There was only a tiny staircase to the fire escape!

"How could anybody leave more than thirty people trapped in a burning warehouse to die?" Korir wondered. The workers were busy packing cocaine into small one kilo packets labelled: 'Original Kenyan Coffee', oblivious of what was happening.

"These warehouses cum factories in Viwandani Zones need to be investigated," he spurted from his clenched teeth. "Dubious business is going on. The workers are poor and they know what they are doing is illegal but they have no other source of income."

"Anybody callous and cold-blooded enough to leave people to die in a burning warehouse would have no compunction about killing me. If I got in their way; not even Kadzo and Kenga would be spared. These people have killed before and would do it again!"

The sirens of fire engines disrupted Korir's thoughts. The firemen managed to put out the fire; a few people got mild burns on their hands and feet and were rushed to hospital.

* * *

After two hours on the road from the Bonded TransCargo Warehouse, it became clear to Inspector Korir that Kadzo knew where they were headed. It became even clearer to him as she gave instructions that the transfer was to be made in the high seas a few hundred miles north of Watamu. In the low-slung cockpit of the Sonic Police Unit motor launch, Kadzo navigated out to sea on a south-easterly heading.

"This bait-girl-bait-boy team of brother and sister knows this ocean well," thought Inspector Korir.

They stopped talking as they could not hear one another well because of the rush of wind and the hollow boom of the speedboat's hull against the swell. The Inspector's admiration of Kadzo grew when she calmly told him that they were meeting up with a freighter, most probably as they had done countless of times before to offload cocaine and heroin onto their speedboat. Big Man had told her and Kenga to be here at this time to do the same job they had done the previous day with the thirty carcasses of sharks. The freighter would be coming in from the south and their launches range was now no more than two hundred miles.

Inspector Korir had ordered for the only available police coast guard helicopter to follow Kadzo's navigation. The chopper flew over the blue ocean and followed them at a distance not to arouse any suspicions. A large distinctive silhouette appeared off the starboard horizon; it was a freighter as Kadzo had said, low in the water, ploughing a northerly course against the current. It proved that Kadzo's navigating was spot on – the drills by Big Man, of memorising instructions on meeting and drop-off points were coming in handy. She had not gone even a quarter of a mile off radar!

The MV Indigo was a twenty-year old former Russian-registered grain freighter, now registered as transporting sugar and *mtumba* clothes around the East African coast. The hulk of the ship was now patiently anchored in the Kenyan high seas, waiting to offload two hundred kilogrammes of cocaine onto the Safari Hatua. His illicit cargo worried him sometimes but not too much. After all, people understood that an old out-of-work captain like him needed to make some money. His regular stops at Rabat, Libreville and Maputo were generally patrolled by an official with a peaked cap, shiny badge and white uniform who would let you bomb his own country for a few US dollars. But that was all before 9/11 and the War on Terror.

Now, even in these godforsaken places, it was common for you to be anchored in the high seas and still have the FBI and CIA swarming your vessel searching for rocket launchers and Al-Qaeda and Al-Shabaab stowaways! Mombasa, or rather the Kenyan coast was one port of call where he could breathe easy, thanks to Mustapha Jillo aka Big Man aka Mono-eye. If only all the African port officials were in the pockets of such barons, business would be good for both the moguls with capital and the hustlers without a penny. He was always punctual and he was already here in his own speedboat waiting for his two African kids.

In the meantime, Inspector Korir's eyes were fixed on the looming hulk of the freighter. He was amazed again at the calmness of Kadzo and Kenga. These kids were used to this drama! Even after the shark attack, Kadzo was still willing to navigate them to meet this freighter yet she was still afraid of diving into the ocean with abandon, the way she used to do before.

At that very moment, the Italian skipper sensed something was wrong because it was not Safari Hatua as Big Man had told him but a police launcher skimming the water towards them. He hurriedly tried to pick anchor but Kadzo slammed the throttles forward as far as they could go. The confused skipper hesitated as the massive Cobra 1100-horsepower engines brought the police launcher to within collision distance with his ship. The hesitation was enough for Inspector Korir to climb up the ladder to the MV Indigo's massive hull, followed by the other officers. The sonic was now anchored between the two lips of MV Indigo's wake and crested the swell left by the huge freighter. As the cops and Kadzo and Kenga came on board, Captain Andressano panicked.

"I've just discovered that I have two hundred kilos of cocaine disguised as shark meat in the hold of my ship and I have no idea how it got there! This gentleman here and his goons have just hijacked my ship!" he shouted pointing at Big Man and two stevedores who were beside him.

Big Man gestured for him to keep quiet whispering to him that as plan B, he always had a seaplane waiting for him about fifty clicks north at Kipini and they could use it to escape. The skipper did not pay attention but went on blabbering.

"Kindly, move forward with your hands raised up," a voice from behind calmly stated.

The Italian skipper turned and stared at the Kenyan officers standing by the ladder of the cabin door and then at Korir who stepped forward.

"My name is Inspector Korir of the Kenya Anti-Narcotics Unit."

"Cops?" the skipper stared incredulously at Big Man.

"We are here because of the cargo in the hold of your ship captain: that you've just so obligingly confessed to."

"As I've just told you, I had no idea that these narcotics had been smuggled aboard my ship until this goon and his pirates hijacked me in the high seas and forced me into the Kenyan waters. I didn't understand what they wanted at first as I only have sugar aboard my ship. However, upon conducting an inventory, that's when I realised what they were after!" the skipper said as he smiled widely.

Inspector Korir shifted his eyes from the short middle-aged pot-bellied Italian skipper in front of him to the one-eyed man standing beside him. Korir's mind went back to his second meeting with the man who had multiple passports. Then he had both of his eyes intact. That time, Inspector Korir was investigating a fake passports cartel in Nairobi.

"It's a small world Inspector," Big Man burst out startling the cautious inspector from his concealed thoughts.

"That's Kenya for you," Korir countered. "You just keep running into the same people in the same criminal circles all the time. Can I ask you a question?" he continued.

"Please, do."

"What exactly do you do for a living Big Man, Mustapha?"

"Didn't I tell you that a couple of years ago when we first met? That time you were accusing me of being behind a spate of carjacking and I told you that I'm an entrepreneur? The truth is, I've done lots of things in my life. I've had a number of jobs. Perhaps I don't know what it is I want to do, really. A few years ago, I thought I had all the time in the world to make up my mind but time has this weird habit of passing pretty fast. That is when you start to panic and wonder about your function in life."

"Is this a roundabout way of saying that you are unemployed?"

"Unemployed but not poor. I hope you understand what I'm saying. I finally found something lucrative and you should join me as a partner. There is, of course, another solution to all this ..."

"What?"

It was now four years since the previous encounter with Big Man and Korir was finding himself in the same position of being offered the same solution but this time, in the hold of a freighter he was inspecting. He was alone with Big Man and a few inexperienced corporals who would be none-the-wiser should Korir accept Big Man's offer. Just like the other time, the bling glinting from Big Man's neck and fingers was enough to make one go blind. Short and well built, he was in his usual colourful shirts and shorts which hung several inches below his bonny knees as if they were made for someone else. Big Man opened a briefcase full of crisp new one thousand shilling notes. He picked up a bundle and waved it under Korir's nose.

"Don't be stupid like the other time. Let me go and all this will be yours. It's only a couple of million shillings but there is more where this came from."

Inspector Korir had learnt the hardest way that corruption reigns supreme in this coastal paradise as far as narcotics were concerned. He had heard of how police officers who were transferred to this place while walking on foot soon drove Mercedes Benz' and became landlords with several estates to their names – an amazing overnight transformation and an impossible feat to achieve with the peanuts they earned as salaries.

Inspector Korir understood why it was said that *Kitu Kidogo* had become a tradition in the force. Clean cops like him were fighting a losing battle. Magistrates who passed heavy sentences on drug barons and traffickers were transferred to hardship areas to wrestle with bandits and cattle rustlers. He made up his mind. He had to arrest this criminal there and then and ensure that Big Man was not granted bail or bond as he would most likely abscond and leave the country! What was he to do?

The off-spring of the generation that had refused to embrace nationalism had looted people's land and as if that was not enough, they had gone ahead to become drug barons, mercilessly snuffing out life from young people. Law enforcers targeted the petty drug users and peddlers while they protected these drug lords. This is why prisons were full of these petty offenders while the barons expanded their businesses and real estate property along the lucrative coastal line. They could also spare funds to invest and open accounts abroad. Korir was in a tight situation but two teenagers had infected him with their enthusiasm to fight this monster called "drug trafficking." He was not about to let them down by giving up or compromising his integrity!

Korir was surprised that Kadzo had been right and Big Man was too greedy to let this consignment slip from his fingers – his escape from the warehouse had brought him straight here!

* * *

In an hour's time, Big Man, his stevedores, Captain Andressano and his crew of six were put into the police launch. From the freighter, the detectives recovered 2000 kilogrammes of cocaine, several satellite phones, four pistols and 200 bullets. Kadzo was glad that she had done her best to help Inspector Korir and his colleagues carry out this sting operation. They had planned for operation for three weeks as they awaited the past couple of days' huge consignments.

Chapter Twenty four

"Sir, Mustapha Jillo aka Mono-eye aka Big Man kept a record of all the cops he had in his pocket."

"I see," the county police boss tried to act cool. "Where did you find this record Inspector; how can you be so precise that it is a true and accurate account?"

"As you well know, Sir, Big Man has been in custody for only three days and last night, he and some members of his cartel escaped from police custody again," Korir said as he bent towards his boss.

"It beats me how he could fall sick in his cell in the middle of the night, be rushed to the hospital and then escape in handcuffs! Anyway," he rose to upright position, "I managed to get some records from his office at his warehouse before it burned down," Korir said as he put his hand in his pocket as if to remove a list of names.

"Thanks to the brave girl, Kadzo, and her brother, Kenga, we came to know about the cargo that was to be transported three nights ago and we laid a dragnet," Korir now wore a scornful sneer.

"Your name is the first on the list, Sir. Should anything untoward happen to me, I have taken the liberty of forwarding this list to the National Police Boss. I have updated him on my investigations and the logical conclusions that I've come to from this list."

"Anything untoward such as, Inspector?"

"Such as what happened to my partner, Sergeant Bilal, who was murdered in cold blood in a bid to silence him."

"Silenced? Wasn't it a carjacking gone wrong? Silenced by whom?"

"By you, Sir. And of course, you know that it wasn't a carjacking otherwise his car would have been stolen. Even his wallet with a few thousand shillings was left intact on him."

Korir watched as his boss' eyes almost popped out of their sockets when he glanced at the list on the table; his eyes transfixed in a trance at the first name on the list.

"Are you out of your mind, Inspector? Do you know the accusations you are making are very serious? And it seems that you have everything worked out, Inspector."

"Yes, Sir. I have. Big Man kept it well-documented and verbal testimonies by witnesses that show that such offers of cash were made to you Sir, are available on record. We also have CCTV footage of you receiving payments in our possession," Korir added.

"Also, in Inspector Bilal's concluding investigations before he died, he indicated that the ship that blew up at sea resulting in Kadzo being attacked by the shark was a bombing and not an accident caused by a faulty fuel leak as some of the officers you assigned the case initially deduced; something to do with concealing of evidence. But I assure you, Sir, that one of these days, I will get Big Man. Even if from my investigations I've discovered that he is a philanthropist to his community and he is always kind and generous to a fault, he will have to face the law; philanthropist or no philanthropist. He is a tough profile to arrest because no one talks ill of him and the bottom line is that even if he were arrested, no one will be willing to testify against him. But I swear I will get him."

"You young cops think that you know everything," the boss said as he stood up. "Be very careful, Korir. If you remember well, after Bilal attempted to confront this so-called Big Man on his own, he died mysteriously."

Chapter Twenty five

K adzo made her way slowly to the microphone mounted near the podium. It had become easier for her to walk because she had gotten used to her artificial leg. Her right leg had mended well and stopped aching. She looked at the many assembled guests seated under tents on the lawn of the King's House. The president was here and she was reading her speech. She had a few minutes earlier interacted with other deserving Kenyans who were being awarded the Head of State Commendation among other presidential awards. When she saw her mother, father, Kenga, Issa, Jamila and their parents seated with Inspector Korir, she felt more confident. Kadzo started to read her essay and her magnified voice boomed from the loud speakers spaced strategically in the corners of tents.

"Though the topic for the essay competition was: THE KENYA I DO NOT WANT TO LIVE IN, mine is also a letter to our President," Kadzo's clear voice penetrated the audience.

"Drug abuse is the non-medical use of drugs that destroys the health and productive life of an individual. Drug and substance abuse in our country, especially among young people of my age, has reached an alarming state. I am one of these young people who was once addicted to drugs. I did not only use but also peddled them. As a result, I lost my leg in a shark attack – most of you must have heard about my escapades in the news.

Kenya has become an international gateway and transit point for drug trafficking. It is now officially the arena for trans-shipment and re-packaging of cocaine and heroin. This is the Kenya I do not want to live in. As I write this essay, I am ashamed that I was once part of this notoriety though not anymore. I want us to join hands to reclaim Kenya's pride. The everyday arrest of petty drug peddlers is symptomatic of how deep the cancer of corruption has made our borders and other entry points porous. Corruption has made our law enforcement agencies weak-kneed and anti-drug trafficking agencies pliable to manipulation from the perpetrators of this illegal trade.

The drug barons have developed sophisticated methods of ferrying their illicit merchandise. They have sucked into their vortex the police, other law enforcers and top people in government and the political class. This is the Kenya I do not want to live in. Through this essay, I call upon the country's leadership to tackle this drug problem. To make matters worse is the issue of unemployment, terrorism, piracy and inadequate housing. Take terrorism for example, reports indicate that some youth in my county have been recruited to join the Al Shabaab militia. Mombasa County is a hub and conduit for the drug trade. Heroin and cocaine find easy access through the old port and *panya* routes. More than 30 per cent of people countrywide are on one form of substance abuse or the other. The coastal counties alone have so many heroin addicts. My country Kenya is listed alongside other countries as having the highest number of opiate users in Africa. This is certainly the Kenya I do not want to live in. It is estimated that there are between 100,000 and 1.3 million users, mostly of heroin in East Africa alone. It is a worrying statistic. Kenya is among the leading nations in injection drug use. To make matters worse, a larger percentage of the Kenyan injecting drug users are HIV positive. This habit has increased the HIV prevalence and brought immense poverty to families because the addicts steal to finance the habit.

It has been estimated that each heroin addict needs approximately 600 shillings a day to satisfy their dependency. This amounts to millions of shillings a day, spent on heroin alone in the region. Unfortunately, drug and substance abuse has become an acceptable part of our coastal culture. Mama mboga and sweet vendors peddle hard drugs just as I did and I also know some of my school mates who are given bhang by their parents to sell to fellow classmates in order to pay their schools fees. This is definitely the Kenya I do not want to live in.

Distribution centres and networks are well known even to the police officers who are complicit in the whole trade. I know this because I was once used to supply drugs and only recently did I get reformed. If all Kenyans think the way I do, I would like to have a more accountable and honest police force; enforcing law and order in my country.

Our country does not produce cocaine or heroin. How then can we explain the fact that our country is routinely the fertile ground on which shipment after shipment of these two substances is netted? Where do they come from? How do they get into Kenya? Whose responsibility is it to stop the entry and re-exportation from our mother land? The solution does not lie with the National Assembly, the Central Government or the County Government which are most of the time, dilly dallying. The solution is with us. People power!

Ahem! The solution to solving this problem lies squarely with our religious leaders and the local community. We need political will and resolve. We also need the social and personal will and resolve to fight the menace. A Kenya in which all the people being looked upon by the citizens fold their hands, leaving the masses vulnerable in the hands of the merciless drug barons is the Kenya I do not want to live in but if the following measures are taken, then it will be the Kenya I want to live in. Drug and substance abuse should be declared a national disaster in order to be adequately addressed.

Each school in the country should have a teacher trained in drug and substance abuse counselling. The Ministry of Education should put in place mechanisms to ensure that all schools are drug-free zones. This should be done by ensuring that schools are fenced off, strangers are kept out and drug abuse education programmes are initiated. Children, teens or young adults programmes in the country should have a trained drug and substance abuse counsellor. Institutions should also be trained to initiate and offer professional courses related to drug and substance abuse. This then will be the Kenya we all want to live in.

To my age-mates, do not be lured by your peers to indulge in drug abuse in order to feel macho which may be exciting in the short run but ruins your entire life – to feel macho you can just play football and win in the local league or be a swimming champion just like me!

To our parents, please, open communication channels with us, your children. All we need is for you to create time and talk to us. Teach us resilience skills and correct our misperceptions and misconceptions on drugs and the consequences of their use. Where I come from – Mombasa County which is hardest hit by drug abuse among the youth, there are only a few rehabilitation centres – we clearly need more rehabilitation centres, Your Excellency. And above all Your Excellency, you as our President should lead this fight against drug trafficking and drug abuse by starting to clean up any drug barons who might be sitting in this audience today or on the podium with you but masquerading as MPs or cabinet secretaries. These drug barons are like the shark which attacked me – they are sharks attacking our youth!

This is the end of my essay but I want to say that the Ministry of Education officials slightly doctored and edited my speech, especially the last sentence which was all together deleted but I had the original one in my pocket, that is what I have read. Thank you."

The audience responded with a standing ovation and thunderous applause. Some government officials seated at the podium fidgeted uncomfortably but Kadzo had already put a finger on the point.

* * *

A newspaper headline a day later with a short article read as follows:

"TRIPLE WIN FOR DRUGS HEROINE"

"Pardon the intended pun in our sub-headline today. Kadzo Karisa, the feisty former teenage drug addict and peddler is today a triple winner having helped the police bust a drug cartel, though the main drug baron has escaped from police custody in unclear circumstances. She won first prize in the national essay writing competition and to cap it all, received a Head of State Commendation. Kadzo read her winning essay in speech form to the President at King's House Nairobi, to the embarrassment of an uncomfortable cabinet and national assembly. Secondary school students were asked to write an essay entitled 'The Kenya I do Not Want to Live In'. Kadzo used her experiences in the drugs underworld to capture the attention of the entire country."

* * *

At the Sea View Restaurant, overlooking the Nyali Creek Seafront, Kadzo and Kenga were hosted to a celebratory dinner. Kadzo's favourite king prawns and lobsters were on the main course. The world-famous Tamarind Dhow was moored and bobbing by the waters of the pier. Present was her family, neighbours, teachers, fellow students, her swimming coach and her swim mates from the Coast Aquatic Swimming Club who had continuously offered her support in her quest to go back to competitive swimming despite having lost one leg.

Perched precariously in his upgraded seat at the front of the police Buffalo aeroplane, Korir who had just left the party, was having an overhead tour of his new jurisdiction. Korir had recently been promoted to Police Boss, Mombasa County. He stared out of his window at the panoramic view of the coastal archipelago below. He was seated with the pilot near the cockpit. He had fallen in love with Mtwapa Creek which nestles between Mombasa and Kilifi counties. This cop was considering settling here. Despite the months spent at the coast, he still hated the thought of swimming in the sea. He had never even dipped his foot into a swimming pool.

* * *

The sheer vastness of the blue ocean with no land in sight terrified him but he was slowly getting used to it. He was amazed at how these two kids handled the waves and dove into the belly of the ocean, Kadzo especially! It was her maiden dive into the depths of the sea since the shark attack. She was attempting to beat the sea-phobia she had fallen prey to! He watched from the plane as she dove into the vast ocean.

Kadzo was now an official tour guide for hire over the school holidays at the Shimoni Caves. She charged three hundred shillings per guided tour instead of being a bait girl for dubious characters. She had recruited several other teenagers and they used the funds they raised to sustain the rehabilitation centre she had initiated.

The vast ocean startled her momentarily. In the past, she always took the presence of the blue sea for granted because it was always there as she ran her daily errands. The status quo changed after the shark attack incident. This great mass of water, whose colour changed from ash-grey to emerald-green and from azure-blue to ink-black was an amazement. Even the wind stiffening her clothes, the mist rushing through her corn-rowed hair, the salt dusting her skin and the wind threatening to push her over into the sea now that she only had one strong leg, were a wonder. Before, she had taken all this as ordinary happenings. She now dove to the belly of the sea and bumped into a colony of intricate lavender and swam through a school of calamari that broke apart at her intrusion and then rejoined into one school once her fleeting presence was gone.

She stroked further past a terrace of black brain corals to the sandy floor. She found a Stingray almost hidden in the sand, its yellow eyes flashing with irritation. With a fluff of its iron grey wing-like fins, the Stingray was in fast flight as the sand that hid it floated away like smoke. The first surge from the Stingray took her by surprise but she managed to dodge its deadly arsenal. She remembered how they had heard on CNN that an Australian naturalist died of Stingray stings. She had not succumbed to a shark attack – was a mere Stingray going to end her life?

The angry being gave up trying to sting her and in all its sovereignty, glided to the bottom gently until the sandy floor settled over it and covered it again. In a split second, a plaque of Stingrays majestically soared in from nowhere. They wrestled against Kadzo in a thrall of motion, their tails frantically flaring against her flesh, showing their white undersides and toothless mouths which looked as if they wore a smile. They jostled onto her back and held her under them. Kenga came to her rescue and churned the water with his legs, fighting off the Stingrays. As she swam to the surface for a breath of air, Kadzo believed that she was truly finally over her shark-sea-phobia and she was going to do her best to achieve the goals she had set for herself. She would start by writing a book entitled *The Shark Attack.*

Glossary

Adhuhuri **prayers**	prayers made at noon by Muslims
Afadhali muishie	you better leave
Allâh	name for God in Islam
Backstroke	a style of swimming where the swimmer lies on their back
Bara	mainland; far away from the coast
Baraza	a meeting
Biryani	fried rice mixed with meat
Cockpit	part of an aeroplane where the pilot and the co-pilot sit
Decipher	be able to make up meaning
Deck	a flat part of a ship where people walk on
Debris	broken or damaged pieces that remain after something has been destroyed
Flippers	flat wide rubber shoes worn to help a swimmer swim faster
Freighter	a large cargo ship
Henchmen	people who support powerful people in committing crime
Hull	part of the ship which is usually above the water surface

Leo haunipambi?	Are you not treating me today?
Mashua	wooden boat usually rowed by use of paddles
Mbuzi	a traditional tool used to grate coconuts
Miraa	khat
Mji wa Kale	old town
OP	abbreviation for outpatient (a patient who receives medication from a hospital and does not stay in a hospital ward
Radar	a system which determines location of an aeroplane or ship by use of radio signals
Safari Hatua	a journey begins with a single step
Salah	prayer
Seaboard	the part of a land or country that borders the sea
Stern	the back part of a ship
Stevedores	someone who puts and removes cargo from a ship at a dock
Stingray	a large flat fish which can sting
Tashbih	beads used by Muslims during prayer
Tibia	a bone located at the front part of the lower leg

Wananchi   citizens

Zii   no

Tafadhali nisikilizeni! Kindly listen to me

Huyu sweba wako ni mwera?

                Is your friend a cop?

Hii maneno itaangaliwa.

                This issue will be looked into

Mazee! Hii ni noma. Buda atazusha

                I say. This is quite serious. Father will be so
                angry

Jameni! watoto wamezubaa hawa! Hili ni janga kuu!

                Our children have become zombies! This is a
                disaster!

Hawa watoto wa matajiri ni watoro shuleni, wanakuja huku mbali kujificha, wavute bhangi na watumie unga na madawa mengine ya kulevya.

                These children from rich families cut
                classes and come this far to hide and smoke
                Marijuana, use cocaine and other illicit drugs.

Sisi tumechoka bwana! Watoto wetu wamekuwa waizi kwa sababu hawana pesa za kununua unga. Unga kama ukucha ni shillingi mia mbili. Wasichana wanakuwa malaya na wavuluna mashoga ili tu wapate ndong'a

                We are tired! Our children have become
                thieves because they have no money to buy

cocaine. Just a pinch goes for two hundred shillings, our girls have become prostitutes and the boy's homosexuals so that they can just get heroin.

Kila kitu kilikuwa ni mwiko! Mwiko! Mwiko! Kuzungumza na watoto juu ya kufanya mapenzi ni mwiko! Hiki kimya kimezidi! Kuzungumza juu ya ukimwi ilikuwa ni mwiko sasa huu ugonjwa umeaua jamii zetu, sasa pia kuzungumza juu ya madawa ya kulevya ni mwiko?

Everything used to be taboo! taboo! taboo! Discussions about sex to children was taboo! This silence is too much! Talking about AIDS was taboo, now the disease is killing our families, now is it also taboo to talk about these illicit drugs?

Hatutaki hizo ahadi za bure! Tumechoka! Wauzaji mnawashika; mahakamani wanaachiliwa! Mbona hamwakamatii mababe wenye kuleta madawa nchini? Na wenye kuwalipa vijana waauze huu unga?

We do not want your false promises! We are tired! You always arrest these petty peddlers; in court they are set free! Why don't you apprehend the drug barons who bring the drugs into the country? What about the people who finance these young peddlers?

Huyu msichana shupavu ndiye anayeongoza maandamano haya. Unaona alipoteza mguu baharani kwa papa akijihusisha na madawa ya kulevya? Lakini amewacha anataka kuwasaidia wenzake! Wewe utafanya nini kumaliza jinamizi hili la ndonga

This courageous and bold girl is the organiser of this demonstration. You can see that she lost a leg to a shark attack at sea while peddling drugs? She has now reformed and wants to help the other kids? What are you doing to eradicate this drug menace?

Printed in the United States
By Bookmasters